DOCTOR WHO

AND THE PIRATE PLANET

DOCTOR WHO

AND THE PIRATE PLANET

This Target novelisation, *Doctor Who and the Pirate Planet*, is based on the 1978 TV story. For a version based on Douglas Adams's first draft scripts, check out BBC Books' *Doctor Who – The Pirate Planet*. It's a much longer – and very different – book.

JAMES GOSS

BOOKS

1

BBC Books, an imprint of Ebury Publishing
20 Vauxhall Bridge Road,
London SW1V 2SA

BBC Books is part of the Penguin Random House group of companies
whose addresses can be found at global.penguinrandomhouse.com

Penguin
Random House
UK

First published by BBC Books in 2017
This edition published by BBC Books in 2021

www.penguin.co.uk

A CIP catalogue record for this book is available from the British Library

ISBN 9781785945304

Editorial Director: Albert DePetrillo
Project Editor: Steve Cole
Cover design: Two Associates
Cover illustration: Anthony Dry
Production: Sian Pratley

Typeset in 11.4/14.6 pt Adobe Caslon Pro
by Integra Software Services Pvt. Ltd, Pondicherry

Printed and bound in Great Britain by Clays Ltd, Elcograf S.p.A.

The authorised representative in the EEA is Penguin Random House Ireland,
Morrison Chambers, 32 Nassau Street, Dublin D02 YH68.

Penguin Random House is committed to a sustainable future for
our business, our readers and our planet. This book is made
from Forest Stewardship Council® certified paper.

Contents

Chapter One

The Sky with Diamonds

They were already calling for Mr Fibuli. Voices echoed through the entire Citadel, drifting down the mountain to the city below, out over the desolate plains beyond, until it seemed that the entire planet of Zanak knew that the Captain wanted to see Mr Fibuli. And when the Captain wanted to see Mr Fibuli, it was never good news.

The Captain (who cannot yet be described) was sitting in his chair (which can). The Captain's chair was large and black and could spin round very quickly if its occupant needed to do some angry glaring. As he needed to do this frequently, it was kept very well oiled.

'Mr Fibuli!' he bellowed. 'By all the X-ray storms of Vega, where is that nincompoop?'

The Captain's Nurse (who was meekly adept at keeping herself out of the way) made a note to check his blood sugar. The drive operators were glad the shouting was not aimed at them. The sifting technicians shrugged.

'Moons of madness, why am I encumbered with incompetents?!'

No one answered this. The Captain rarely expected an answer to that sort of question. A fussy little man in a drab uniform came hurrying onto the Bridge.

'Captain, sir!' he announced, sighing to a halt before the back of that large black chair.

'Your report, Mr Fibuli?' The voice that emerged from the chair was silken.

Mr Fibuli ran a tongue around his mouth in a futile search for moisture. 'Yes … I have it …'

'It's thirty seconds late.'

'Yes, sir.'

'My qualities are many, Mr Fibuli,' rumbled the chair.

'Oh yes, sir!'

'But I'm afraid an infinite capacity for patience is not one of them.'

Choosing his moment, the Captain spun round in his chair and, since he did so, we may as well finally describe him. If his chair was imposing and covered with wires, then the Captain was rather more so. It was hard to tell where the chair ended and the Captain began. Nestled amongst it all were the remains of a very large man. Half of his face was covered with a metallic plate. A green eyepatch glowed dangerously, metal lips sneered, and even half of his beard was iron. Things got worse beneath the neck. A vast robotic arm, two

2

artificial legs, synthetic lungs that hissed with effort, and, at the end of a velvet-covered sleeve, the rather pathetic remains of a human hand twitched.

There wasn't much of the Captain left, but still more than enough to be absolutely terrifying. What did not help was the smell. Wafting around the Captain, especially when he was angry, was the odour of slowly cooking meat.

'I apologise most abjectly, Captain, sir, but I do believe I have good news, sir.'

'I hope you do.'

Something was scuttling across the Captain's shoulder, shifting its weight from one metal claw to another. It too was glaring at Mr Fibuli.

'Well, sir, all deposits of the minerals Voolium, Galdrium and Assetenite 455 have now been mined, processed and stored. We have lots of Silicates, Alumina, Carbon Isotopes, et cetera, etcetera, and the residue has, you will be pleased to hear, been processed.'

'In the normal way?'

'Yes, sir. The Captain's seemed a strange preoccupation, but then again, theirs was a strange life, and every man must have his hobby. 'Oh, and here is a list of the minerals, sir.'

The Captain took the list, glanced at it and let it slide from his mechanical grasp. 'Ha! Baubles, baubles, dross and baubles!' With a grunt of pistons, he leaned forward in his chair, his diesel breath wafting over

Mr Fibuli. 'We must find Vasilium. We must find Madranite 1–5!'

'Well, sir …' Mr Fibuli, flicking through his printouts, smiled. 'We have located a new source.'

'Excellent.' The Captain clucked with delight, as did the creature on his shoulder.

The Captain's pet was almost as unpleasant as he was. It killed people quickly (sometimes) and painfully (always). It was a small robot parrot. Its eyes were bloody diamonds, its sharp plumage a spread of precious metals, its claws and beak titanium. At first glance you might have said, 'How cute,' but then you wouldn't have got a second glance. The gimlet eyes of the creature drilled into Mr Fibuli and told him quite plainly that he was about to die.

'That's what caused my delay. I wanted to be absolutely certain …' Aware he was babbling, Mr Fibuli fished among the papers in the crook of his arm, and pulled out what he hoped was the correct map. 'Let me show it to you on this chart. You see the source is in a very unexpected sector of space …'

The Captain didn't even glance at the details. 'We'll mine it! Make immediate preparations.'

Mr Fibuli continued to look at the star charts and frowned. The problem with the source was that it really shouldn't have been there. 'Well, there is something rather curious. Here's a detailed description of the sector …'

The Captain stood with a hydraulic growl. 'I said, we'll mine it, Mr Fibuli!'

'But …' Mr Fibuli often wondered if 'but' would be his last word.

The Captain's mechanical arm swung out, swatting Mr Fibuli away. 'Make immediate preparations now, or I'll have your bones bleached.'

'Aye, aye, Captain, thank you, sir,' whispered Mr Fibuli as he scurried from the room. For the Captain's crew were not only pirates, they were efficient ones.

The Captain leaned forward and bellowed into a microphone.

'People of Zanak! Now hear this! This is your Captain speaking …"

Down in the streets of Zanak, blowing out across the dunes, the Captain's voice echoed. The people stopped and listened, partly out of fear, partly out of excitement.

'Citizens, prepare yourselves. Watch for the omens. I declare a new golden age of prosperity for all.'

Some people cheered. After all, they were going to be rich today. Perhaps it would rain diamonds later.

The Captain's voice drifted out across the deserts.

'I say again, I declare the dawning of a new golden age of prosperity. Watch for the omens.'

*

His voice was even heard deep underground, in a cavern as old as the planet. In the chamber, a group of cloaked figures were staring at a glowing patch of air that showed a series of shifting images as it flitted between the eyes of the people of Zanak.

'The mines will once again be full of riches,' boomed the Captain. 'Richer jewels. Finer clothes. Food in greater abundance.'

As his words drifted through the cheering crowds, one man was not celebrating. A young man with a pinched, worried face. The image of him filled the glowing picture in the cave.

As the Captain promised, 'Wealth beyond the dreams of avarice will be yours,' the young man backed away in horror.

The weary eyes of the ancient people in the cavern followed the young man.

'Brothers, are we agreed?' asked one. 'We have found another. The days grow dark. The time of evil is once more come. We must prepare ...'

The Doctor was on a quest, and quests always made him sulky.

The Key to Time may have been the most powerful object in the universe, but the Doctor found it boring. Yes, it could restore the balance between good and evil, but really ... did there have to be six pieces of it?

The Doctor had been assigned the task of collecting the Key to Time by the White Guardian, who, if not exactly God, was certainly happy to fill in for Him if He was busy. So far, the Doctor had collected one piece out of the six and was already thoroughly over the whole business.

His hearts in his boots, the Doctor dreaded slinking around the universe, gradually turning his time machine into a trinket shop stuffed full of crystals, pendants and knick-knacks. It would be terribly embarrassing if he invited people round. Which was unlikely, because of the other annoying thing about the Key to Time.

The other annoying thing about the Key to Time was that the Guardian had given the Doctor a new companion. If asked, the Doctor would have pointed out that he already had the ideal companion. It was a robot dog called K-9, who allowed the Doctor to cheat at chess and ran out of steam when faced with a steep hill. No yomping up mountains with K-9 around, which, considering the Doctor was now knocking at 750, was something of a blessing.

But no, the Guardian had provided him with the Time Lady Romanadvoratrelundar. Fresh out of Gallifrey's Time Lord Academy, she was elegant, intimidating, and about as much fun as a well-dressed telephone directory. The Doctor was quietly terrified of her.

This Doctor, in his fourth body, was a proud spiller of crumbs and defier of conventions. Every morning, he pounced on his wardrobe as though he were seeking revenge. This was a man who woke up, grabbed a scarf, and went to laugh hard at the universe. And right now the Doctor was in a quiet bit of his ship with K-9, polishing the first segment of the Key to Time with said scarf. He wasn't hiding, not as such. He was just hoping Romanadvoratrelundar wouldn't find him.

'There we go, K-9,' he announced, holding the segment up to the light. 'The first segment of the Key to Time. A job well done.'

'Correction, Master.' K-9 was a stickler for detail. 'A job well done to the extent of 0.16666.'

Sometimes the Doctor wondered where K-9 got his numbers from. 'Yes. The others will be easy. A piece of cake.'

'Piece of cake, Master?'

With a casualness that would have made a museum curator gasp, the Doctor tossed the segment in a quantum vault. 'Well ...'

'Piece of cake. Radial segment of baked confection. Coefficient and relevance to the Key to Time, zero.'

'That's what I said, K-9. Piece of cake.'

With a sigh, the Doctor gathered himself together and headed for the control room.

*

The Doctor swept into the central control room of the TARDIS. It was white. Suspiciously whiter than white. Had Romanadvoratrelundar been cleaning? The only thing whiter than the control chamber was Romanadvoratrelundar's dazzling gown. Wherever the Time Lady went, the gown flowed behind her with a slithering grace that tended to scare furniture. She was waiting for him and she was reading a book. Which was ominous. Especially as she'd placed it on a lectern.

'Good morrow, Romana! That looks interesting.'

'Good morning, Doctor.' Romana turned another page and frowned. The frown said, 'I'm not angry, just disappointed.'

'What are you reading?' He had a nasty suspicion.

'Oh, just familiarising myself with the technical details of this capsule.'

'Capsule?' The Doctor fought back the urge to give the controls of his time machine a protective hug. 'Capsule? What kind of a word is that? If you mean TARDIS, why don't you say TARDIS?'

'The Type Forty capsule wasn't on the main syllabus, you see.'

'Not on the syllabus! Ptchah!' The Doctor didn't know what the Academy was coming to these days.

'*Veteran & Vintage Vehicles* was an optional extra.' Romana glanced up from her page, and gave the Doctor a long, cool look. 'I preferred something more interesting.'

'Really? Like what?'

'Oh, the lifecycle of the Gallifreyan flutterwing.'

'Now you're being frivolous.'

'I wouldn't dream of it,' Romana vowed solemnly, and flicked on a little grin the Doctor couldn't help responding to.

He busied himself around the TARDIS console. The Guardian had given him a magic wand for finding the six segments of the Key to Time. He and Romana had discussed what to call it; he'd suggested the Tracer, and of course, she'd plumped for the Locatormutor Core. The Tracer would feed through a series of coordinates, allowing the ship to zero in on the next segment. It was a disappointingly efficient process.

'Hmm,' he said, plugging the Tracer into the console and waiting until it booted up. In practice, this meant going from not glowing at all to sparkling. Exactly like a magic wand. The Doctor found the Tracer deeply embarrassing and handed it over to Romana at every available opportunity. Let her look like a fairy-tale princess.

The Tracer glowed, sparkled, shimmered, and then began to emit coordinates.

'Oh no,' the Doctor tutted. 'How paralysingly dull, boring, and tedious.'

'Our next destination?'

'Yes, Calufrax.'

'Calufrax?' Romana had either never heard of it, or had read the reviews.

'Mean little planet. Still …' The Doctor brightened magnanimously. 'Why don't you watch while I set the coordinates on this vintage veteran of mine? Maybe you'll learn something.'

'Right,' said Romana.

Dismissing a worry that he was being teased, the Doctor moved around the controls of his time machine, inputting the coordinates with the zeal of a concert pianist playing a haunted Wurlitzer organ. If a switch or two popped off, he slipped them into a pocket with the legerdemain of an expert.

He stood back. Job well done. Romana told.

'Er, Doctor?'

'Yes?'

'What about the Synchronic Feedback circuit?'

'What about it?'

'Aren't you going to set it?'

'No, I never bother. Complete waste of time,' he said airily, jamming his hands in his pockets. There did seem to be a lot of broken switches in them. Ah well.

'Only,' Romana said gently, 'according to the manual, it's essential.'

The Doctor decided it was time to give her a friendly bit of advice. Just a hint. 'Listen, have you any idea how long I've been operating this TARDIS?'

'Five hundred and twenty-three years.'

'Right.' Gosh. She was very well informed. 'Is it really that long? My, how time flies.'

'Hasn't it?' Romana said. 'And the Multiloop Stabiliser …'

'What about it?'

Romana was consulting the manual. Of course she was. 'It says here, "On any capsule, it will be found impossible to effect a smooth materialisation without first activating the Multiloop Stabiliser."'

'That's absolute rubbish.' The Doctor tore the page out of the manual, screwed it up, and jammed that in his pocket too. 'Now, I'll show you a really smooth materialisation without a multiloop anything. Watch this.' He pulled a final lever. 'Calufrax, here we come.'

At this point, the TARDIS flung itself around like a sock in a tumble dryer.

'What's happening?' asked Romana, clinging to a wall.

'She won't materialise,' the Doctor yelled, arms wrapped around the time rotor. He could sort this out. Not a problem. 'Just some minor interference on the Vantalla scale. Nothing to worry about.'

'Danger, Master, danger!' announced K-9. Sometimes the robot dog had all the tact of a drunken vicar.

'Of course, of course.' The Doctor tried to wave this away, lost his grip, plunged face first onto the console and ended up spreadeagled on the floor. Given that the floor was at a steep angle, he slid to rest at Romana's feet.

She looked down at him. 'Something wrong?'

'No, no, nothing at all.' The Doctor felt around for his dignity. It was currently missing.

Mr Fibuli felt as though the world was falling apart – which, in the case of the planet Zanak could literally be true. They weren't ordinary pirates, and Zanak was no ordinary planet. The entire Bridge shook and bucked. Mr Fibuli had never been on a rollercoaster but, if you'd explained the concept to him at that moment, he'd have said it just sounded like another bad day at work. And Mr Fibuli had a lot of bad days at work.

Outside the great glass dome, the view of the city beneath them vanished, replaced by a blaze of light.

As the crew were thrown about him, as the control panels exploded, the Captain stood magnificently still, his pet whirling furiously around his head.

'Mr Fibuli!' he raged. 'Thrice worse than incompetent idiots! What pernicious injury have you inflicted on my precious engines?'

Mr Fibuli was scurrying from console to console frantically trying to find out what was happening to the mighty motors of Zanak.

What the Captain said next might've seemed strange to a casual observer.

'Are you trying to scuttle this planet?'

*

Out in the Time Vortex, the TARDIS lurched between existence and non-existence with a speed that would have made Schrödinger's cat sick. Something was terribly wrong – not just with the TARDIS, but with space-time itself.

Chapter Two

Right Place, Wrong Planet

With a final lurch, the planet Zanak stopped shaking. The Captain flung out a hand, plucking Mr Fibuli out of mid air and preventing him from dashing his brains out on a control panel.

'What happened?' the Captain demanded.

Mr Fibuli found himself dangling by the throat, being glared at by both the Captain and his parrot. 'Well—' he began.

'Well?'

Mr Fibuli waved a crumpled set of notes and gestured to the flight computer. 'The actual damage isn't as bad as it looks.'

'Really?' The Captain shook poor Mr Fibuli.

'As far as we can tell, sir, the phenomenon was caused by some freak local disturbance, probably electromagnetic. It passed very quickly.'

The Captain dropped his first mate to the floor. 'Idle prattlings. I will know the truth!' He strode to a charred control panel and plunged his robot arm into it. Sparks formed around it as it interfaced with the systems, and figures flew across a cracked screen.

'There's your local electromagnetic disturbance. What do you make of those readings?'

Mr Fibuli risked a blink. 'Well, that's extraordinary, sir.'

The Captain agreed. For a moment all bluster and fury vanished, replaced by a keen curiosity. 'For ten seconds the entire fabric of the space-time continuum was ripped apart. Critical overload, every system jammed solid. Look at those gravity dilation readings. Can you explain them?'

'Not off the top of my head, sir,' Mr Fibuli admitted.

The Captain nodded, what remained of his lips curling in a smile. 'For ten seconds the whole infrastructure of quantum physics was in retreat.' A metallic eyebrow winched itself up.

'Well—' began Mr Fibuli.

The robot parrot emitted a squawk of outrage. The Captain's Nurse hurried over to his side, keen to check her patient for damage. As she did so, the Captain resumed his former loud manner. 'Find out what happened, Mr Fibuli, and find out fast, or by all the fires of night, I'll have that skull off you!'

In the TARDIS things had assumed the teetering calm of a caravan parked on a precipice.

The Doctor was edging his way towards the control console. 'I am perfectly capable of admitting when I am wrong.'

Romana, he noted, still clung to the wall, even if she clung with the aplomb of someone waiting for canapés to come round. 'Oh really?' she said.

The Doctor slithered a little further forward. Was he imagining the ship shifting with his weight? 'Only this time I wasn't wrong. There was definitely something out there jamming our materialisation field.'

'Oh, that's what it was,' Romana said politely.

'Yes, that's what it was.' The Doctor cautiously sneaked a hand up towards the console, praying the movement wouldn't plunge them into a temporal abyss. 'It was nothing to do with the multiloop whatsit or anything else to do with that manual.'

'No, of course not.' Romana watched his ginger manoeuvres. 'May I try?'

The Doctor had nearly grasped a mergin nut. With a bit of luck, it would give him enough purchase to haul himself up. 'You want to try landing? By the book?'

'Yes,' said Romana, fully aware that the TARDIS manual was in a crumpled heap under the hat stand.

'Why not?' the Doctor said, cautiously raising himself to a crawl. 'You do it your way.'

'Thank you, Doctor,' said Romana. She let go of the wall and strode confidently to the console, flicking at some levers as though they needed dusting.

'You'll see,' the Doctor muttered, winking at K-9. 'There's definitely something out there jamming our materialisation field.'

'Right. Synchronic Feedback set,' Romana announced firmly.

'Won't make a scrap of difference.' The Doctor hated saying 'I told you so.' That was a lie. The Doctor loved doing just that.

'Well, we'll see. Multiloop Stabiliser engaged.' Romana threw the materialisation lever.

The Doctor flung himself away from the console, grabbing hold of his robot dog. 'Hold on K-9, hold on!'

The TARDIS landed soft and sure as a fly on butter.

The Doctor uncurled himself, hardly daring to breathe.

Romana was standing there, watching him coolly. Was she tapping her foot? 'Well?'

'Good,' the Doctor muttered.

'Thank you, Doctor.' Romana helped him up.

The Doctor decided to be magnanimous. Beginner's luck and all that. 'Very promising, wasn't it K-9?'

'It was very, very, very good, Master,' the robot dog announced and the Doctor winced at the betrayal. Still, he had to concede defeat. 'Listen K-9, I know you've been worried about Romana, but I think she's going to be all right. Very all right.'

'Very, very all right,' K-9 decided.

Rising above all this, Romana was checking the external sensors. 'Shall we have a look at Calufrax now?'

'Calufrax? Let's get it over with. Horrible place. Cold, wet, icy. No life of any sort. Boring.'

'It looks very pleasant to me,' announced Romana.

The TARDIS scanner screen was showing a handsome street of pleasant buildings, their sun-soaked plaster glistening with precious stones.

'Calufrax? Pleasant?' the Doctor scoffed. 'You have made an enormous mistake. Probably missed it by a couple of million light years!' He clapped a friendly hand around her shoulders. 'No harm, easily done. Why, the number of times I've ended up on the wrong planet for the right reasons ...'

It was at this point that K-9 starting spinning on the spot and emitting small robotic growls of alarm.

'Oh.' The Doctor frowned. 'I wonder what's biting him?'

Deep in the caverns beneath the planet Zanak, the cowled figures writhed in the dust, their voices chanting in abject misery. 'Life force dying! Life force dying! Life force dying!'

Out in the city, the young man wasn't doing any better. 'Life force dying!' he wailed, running down the street. He didn't see the people backing away from him nervously.

'Life force dying!' he shouted, tumbling into a pile of jewels abandoned on the pavement.

'Life force dying!' He was pounding on a door.

The door was opened by an old man, who stared at him in horror. He grabbed the young man, bundled him inside and slammed the door.

'Life force dying!' the young man cried, writhing on the couch. The old man fussed around him helplessly.

'Calm yourself, Pralix, you must calm yourself.'

A smart young woman, her robes cut in the latest fashion, rushed to the young man's side. She was called Mula, and she had spent her adult life looking after her brother and Balaton, their grandfather. Lately, whenever the Captain declared a New Golden Age of Prosperity, Pralix would fall into a seizure and Balaton would become very, very alarmed. Balaton's family had known more than its fair share of tragedy and he wanted no more of it.

Mula felt Pralix's forehead. 'He's much worse than last time, Grandfather. Pralix, can't you hear us? Tell us what's wrong.'

'Stop asking him! It's a mistake to ask too many questions!'

'That's your answer to everything, isn't it?' Mula loved her grandfather, but he lived in abject fear of everything.

'I have no need for answers, for all I ask is a quiet life.' Balaton glanced nervously at the door, as though worried the Guards would come through and snatch Pralix away – as they'd taken away his father. 'Pralix,

Pralix, you must calm yourself,' he begged, desperately. He fussed away, closing all the windows, hoping no one would hear the sound and report them. 'Are you trying to get us all killed?'

'Life force dying!' Pralix screamed again.

'Strange.' The Doctor was checking the coordinates and staring at the screen. Warm, civilised, distinctly unboggy – everything that Calufrax was not. 'That can't be right. It is right, but it can't be ...'

'Well ...' Romana had taken the Tracer from the control panel and was clearly itching to get out there, collect the next segment and move on. If you left it up to her, the Key to Time would be complete by Wednesday afternoon, and the Doctor had never seen the point of finishing anything on a Wednesday. Especially not when they had a far more interesting mystery to deal with.

'Well, according to these space-time coordinates, we have arrived at precisely the right point in space at precisely the right time.'

'But at the wrong planet,' the Doctor concluded.

Romana paused, curious.

'This isn't Calufrax.' The Doctor strode over to the screen and tapped it. 'I haven't got the faintest idea where we are. All I do know is that this planet wasn't here when *I* tried to land the TARDIS.'

*

A few months ago, Mula had met a nice young man called Kimus. True, he liked himself a bit too much, and enjoyed the sound of his own voice, especially when making speeches about how Something Really Must Be Done About The Captain (if not today then definitely soon). But Kimus did not writhe around screaming every time there was a New Golden Age of Prosperity. So there was that in his favour.

Kimus had arrived at their house to find Pralix wailing on the sofa, Balaton hanging blankets over the windows, and Mula at her wits' end. He'd been hoping for dinner.

'Oh dear, I'm sure people can hear,' Balaton was fussing.

'Pralix is very ill,' Mula was saying patiently. 'And all you can think about is what will happen if the neighbours hear.'

At that moment, she realised Kimus had come in. Balaton stared at him in terror, realised it was him, and skirted round to slam the door shut behind him.

'What's going on?' Kimus asked.

'Life force dying. Life force dying. Life force dying!' shrieked Pralix.

'Oh,' said Kimus. 'That again.'

Pralix's struggles were being watched by the writhing figures in the cavern. An image of him hung above them in the glowing air. Then it dissolved, reforming to show a street on Zanak. And a blue box parked none-too-neatly in the street.

The box opened, and a curly-haired man, a tall woman in a glamorous dress, and a robot dog came out of it.

'We have intruders.' said one of the figures.

The Doctor looked around him. Two suns, a rather steep hill, an appallingly designed citadel on top of the hill, a desert to the left, and a very, very shiny city to the right. This planet was somehow wrong. It looked wrong, it smelt wrong, it felt wrong. Very wrong indeed. Splendid.

Romana took time out from waving the Tracer around to throw him a pitying look. 'So. Calufrax is an uninhabited ice-coated planet?'

The Doctor stuck to his guns. 'Yes.'

'Well, we've certainly come to the right place,' said Romana as the Tracer emitted a fierce crackling. 'The Second Segment is definitely around here. The signal's coming from ...' a tiny frown ... 'everywhere.'

'Never trust gimmicky gadgets, isn't that right, K-9?'

The robot dog cleared his throat. 'Sentient life forms approaching.'

'Calufraxians?' Romana smiled as two people entered the street. 'I thought you said this planet was uninhabited.'

23

'It is.' The Doctor looked at them. Ordinary-enough humanoids wearing cloaks as studded with jewels as their buildings.

'I'll go and talk to them,' Romana suggested.

'No, no.' The Doctor liked enthusiasm, but it had a time and a place. 'I'll deal with it.' He strode towards the two people, hand outstretched, brightest grin on his face. 'Excuse me. Would you mind taking me to your leader. What we'd like to know, you see, is what planet is this?'

The two strangers regarded the Doctor with polite embarrassment and moved on. Seeing some more people at the end of the street, the Doctor raced up to them and repeated his attempts. He was again rebuffed.

'Oh dear,' the Doctor said. 'You're not doing very well at this, K-9.'

'I have a suggestion,' said K-9. 'Allow the Mistress to make contact.'

Romana bowed.

'Nonsense,' the Doctor tutted. 'Making contact with an alien race is an immensely skilled and delicate operation. It calls for tact and experience. What would she know about it?' He noticed another man turn into the street and waved at him frantically.

Romana strode up to the man, tossed back her head and stuck out her hand. 'Hello. Excuse me.'

The man stopped walking and smiled at her. 'Hello!'

The Doctor scowled.

'She is prettier than you, Master,' said K-9.

'Is she?' The Doctor blinked. 'What's that got to do with it?'

K-9 said nothing.

The man was enthusiastically explaining the world to Romana.

'Do go on,' she giggled.

'Well, you see,' gushed the man, 'It's a new Golden Age. A Golden Age of Prosperity. I must say, I still get very excited about it all. I know we have them rather often now, but that's because of the Captain's great goodness, you see.'

'Excuse me, the Captain?' the Doctor tried to cut in.

The man ignored him.

'The Captain?' The Doctor could have sworn that Romana fluttered her eyelashes when she spoke.

'Oh yes! The Captain does it all for us. And it was terribly spectacular this time. Oh yes, the omens! The skies shook like lightning. And you know what that means?'

'No, I'm terribly afraid I don't.' Romana appeared to be using a strange, breathless tone. Perhaps she was having trouble adjusting to the planet's atmosphere. But that wouldn't explain why she was twirling a finger in her hair.

'Oh, well ...' The man grinned. 'It means we're going to be very rich!'

'What, just like that? Rich! Because of lights in the sky? Fancy!' Romana's wide eyes looked terribly impressed.

'That's the way it always happens,' the man said. 'Here, let me give you some diamonds—' The man handed her some precious stones. 'Oh, and a ruby. Suit a pretty girl like you.'

'Why, thank you.' Romana slipped the stones into a pocket and brought out a small paper bag. 'I say, would you like a jelly baby?'

The man helped himself while the Doctor boggled. Now she was stealing his best material. This was only Day Two. Give her a fortnight and it would be 'Hello! I'm Romana and this is my assistant, the Doctor.' He glanced down. K-9 had trundled over to Romana's side. Traitor.

The man ignored the dog, holding a jelly baby up to the light. It glowed a strange green and was rather like a squishy precious stone. 'What are they?' He took four of them, just in case they were valuable.

'Sweets,' announced Romana grandly, then faltered. 'I think you have to eat them or something.'

'Oh, I'll try that,' announced the man uncertainly.

'Excuse me,' the Doctor tried again.

The man popped the jelly baby in his mouth and chewed gently. He broke into a radiant grin. 'I'd better go,' he said, 'or I'll be late for the feast. Nice to have met you. Hope the Mentiads don't get you.'

'Who?' Romana asked. But the man had gone.

The Doctor turned to Romana. 'What I'd like to know is where did you get those jelly babies from?'

'Same place you get them,' she announced. 'Your pocket.' And she dropped them neatly back into his coat with a pat.

Standing on a mysterious alien planet feeling thoroughly outwitted, the Doctor felt it was time to impart a piece of serious moral wisdom. 'Good looks are no substitute for a sound character, you know.'

Romana took the reproof with a nod that was just a shade too grave to be serious. She was chewing slowly on a jelly baby.

The Doctor changed the subject. 'Didn't that man say something about omens?'

'Yes, omens in the sky.' Romana nibbled the head off another sweet.

'Really?' The Doctor made a succession of his very best Thinking Noises.

Chewing happily, the young man turned a corner and walked into one of the Captain's Guards. Before he could even stammer out an apology, the Guard seized a jelly baby from his hand and held it up to the light.

'Where did you get these?'

Without a moment's hesitation, the man pointed towards Romana.

The Guard nodded. Something was wrong.

*

The Doctor would have agreed with him. He was examining the handful of gemstones Romana had been given. 'I think that these stones are genuine.'

K-9 confirmed his opinion, venturing that the clear stones were diamonds, the red stones were rubies.

The Doctor noticed a glittering pile further down the street and started sorting through it, amazed. 'Extraordinary. The place is littered with precious stones. Diamonds, Andromedan bloodstones, gravel, more diamonds. Don't they have street sweepers?'

'Well, perhaps these stones aren't valuable here, Doctor.' Romana was using the Doctor's telescope to survey the strange building on top of the mountain. Its sheer ugliness made it interesting.

'Diamonds and rubies not valuable?' the Doctor scoffed.

Romana held up a stone that glowed with green. 'What's this one?'

'Oolion, Mistress,' K-9 diagnosed.

The Doctor stared. 'Are you sure?'

'Affirmative. Oolion.'

'Oolion? Now that is rare. That's one of the most precious stones in the galaxy. It only occurs naturally in two places that I know of. Qualactin and Bandraginus Five. Bandraginus Five?' The Doctor's nose wrinkled. 'Where have I heard that mentioned recently?'

Romana was entranced by the stone. The Doctor told her to hold it up to the light of the two suns. The glow inside it burst into a flame that danced within the stone. 'People have murdered for that beauty, ravaged empires for it, and here it is, lying in the streets exactly where I wasn't expecting to find it. I wonder where Calufrax got to?'

The Doctor's pleasure at a mystery had turned into worry. The whole situation was so dazzlingly unlikely it felt like someone was interfering with the universe itself.

Chapter Three

Meeting with Unusual Minds

Pralix was still screaming. His grandfather kept peering out the window to see if anyone was coming.

'Poor Pralix,' said Mula. 'What does it all mean?'

'Why should it mean anything?' Balaton told her. 'It's just the way life is. Accept it.'

That was enough to launch Kimus into one of his speeches. 'Oh yes, praise the Captain, we can have anything we want, can't we, apart from the freedom to think for ourselves. Well, I'd like to know what I'm accepting, old man.'

Balaton shook his head wearily. 'I remember when I was a lad. Things were very different then. You think you have no freedom now? You ought to have been here under old Queen Xanxia. Now, *she* was a tyrant ...'

'Oh, Queen Xanxia, is it?' Kimus didn't have time to be scared by Balaton's old fairy stories.

Mula tried shutting them both up, pleading for quiet for Pralix.

'Quiet?' Kimus was on a roll. 'If you ask me, we've all been quiet for too long, and for what? Pretty clothes? Pockets full of useless trinkets? That isn't what life ought to be about.' He took Mula's hand and smiled at her. Despite herself, she smiled back at him.

Balaton was furious. 'Kimus, you are a dangerous fool. I beg you – don't listen to him, Mula. If you love your brother, you must shelter him, hide him, protect him from the Mentiads. Remember what happened to your father.'

'My father didn't fall into the hands of the Mentiads.'

'No.' Balaton winced at the memory.

'He was shot by the Captain's Guards.'

'To save him from the Mentiads!' Balaton reached out for her. She stepped back. 'At least he died a clean death. It was an act of mercy by the Captain.'

'Mercy?' Mula stared at him, aghast.

'Thank you,' sneered Kimus, 'O merciful Captain, thank you for so kindly having Mula's father shot down in the street like a dog.'

Balaton's face was pained. 'It was a dark day, Kimus. But I would strangle Pralix with my own hands to save him from the Mentiads.'

Deep in their cavern, the cowled figures looked up at the shimmering picture of Pralix shimmering in the air.

Their leader stepped forward. The only difference between him and his brethren was that the leader looked even more miserable. His face was lined, not just with age but with an immense sadness. 'Brothers, our Vigil of Evil is accomplished. The one called Pralix must be harvested. The Time of Knowing shall be soon, and fast upon that shall follow the Time of Vengeance. Vengeance for the crimes of Zanak!'

The figures nodded and filed solemnly out of the cavern. The Mentiads had much to do.

A few streets away, the Doctor was still looking for the planet Calufrax.

'Excuse me.' He had taken to knocking on doors, calling through letterboxes and was now, seemingly, bellowing to an eerily empty street. 'Hello! Has anyone seen a place called Calufrax? It's a sort of planet thing. It's ooh … about 14,000 miles across, you couldn't miss it. Oblate spheroid, cold, covered in ice.'

The Doctor finished speaking and cocked a hand to his ear, listening for any reply.

None came.

'Funny. No one's seen it.'

Romana looked around the street. It was quiet. The kind of quiet that assured you that people were home but ignoring you very hard.

The Life Force is dead!

The scream drifted down the street.

'Well someone's around anyway.' The Doctor was already heading towards the noise.

'*We are all murderers! Murderers!*'

Romana watched the Doctor head off, and started to wonder where she'd brought them.

Mula and Kimus were trying to hold a frantic Pralix down.

Balaton advanced on his hysterical grandchild with a pillow. 'We're done for! They must be nearly here! The Mentiads will take him as they tried to take your father!'

Mula knocked the pillow from his hands. 'We must hide him.'

For once Kimus was on Balaton's side. 'We can't hide him forever, Mula,' he said gently.

'They'll be here any moment,' wailed Balaton.

It was at this point that the doorbell rang.

'We're too late,' Balaton said, his voice a whisper. 'Poor Pralix.' Using the last of his courage, he opened the door and got ready to surrender his grandson.

Standing on his doorstep was the Doctor. 'Excuse me, are you sure this planet's meant to be here?'

Romana hadn't even noticed the Doctor had gone. She was staring up at the sky through the Doctor's telescope. The sky was unusual for a binary system, the clouds weren't quite right, and then there was that building on the mountain which looked exactly as though someone had crashed a spaceship into a castle. That looked promising. She decided she would go there.

She brought the telescope down slightly and then squinted. A face was filling it, staring at her. Romana might not have been travelling with the Doctor for very long, but she had already learned how to recognise A Guard. Oh dear.

The Guard snatched the telescope from her. 'This is a forbidden object.'

'Oh, really?' Romana's reply was cool, although she supposed she was in a certain amount of danger. 'Why?'

'That is a forbidden question. You are a stranger?'

'Well, yes,' Romana managed not to roll her eyes.

'Strangers are forbidden,' growled the Guard. Of course he did.

'Oh, I came with the Doctor,' she breezed as though that answered everything. The Guard started to say something, so she held up a hand. 'Don't tell me – Doctors are forbidden as well?'

'You are under arrest,' said the Guard. 'I must take you to the Citadel.'

'Splendid.' Romana beamed and rubbed her hands together.

There was a stunned pause. Normally prisoners were screaming, pleading and begging to be shot by this point. Instead Romana raised an eyebrow and politely waited.

The Guard seized her by the arms and started to drag her away. Even being dragged, she seemed to glide.

As they rounded a corner, a small grey object shot forwards. Before the Guard had noticed it, Romana's leg shot gracefully out, and hastily nudged the object back into the shadows before it could shoot the Guard with a nose-laser.

'No, you mustn't,' she cried.

The Guard smiled. Finally, she was begging for mercy. Good. 'You dare speak?'

'What I said was, "You mustn't, fetch the Doctor."'

'You're mad,' the Guard snarled, dragging Romana away.

From the shadows, K-9 watched Romana go. If he'd been asked his opinion, he would have stated that getting captured was not necessarily a wise move. Certainly not for the Mistress Romana. It was, after all, only her second trip.

The Captain reached up to the robot parrot that crouched on his shoulder. It was the Captain's confidante, soulmate and one true joy in life. Officially it was the Polyphase Avatron, but the crew refused to call it that out of terror. The Captain's artificial hand ruffled the parrot's metal feathers, each one twanging like piano wire. 'We're surrounded by incompetents, you and I. Incompetents and fools,' he cooed. The bird chirruped in agreement. 'You're my only true friend.' The Captain leaned in and lowered his voice even further. 'Never mind. Not long now. Not long before it's finished and we'll be free.'

Mr Fibuli ruined this moment (as he had so many others) by running up with bad news. 'Captain! Captain, sir!'

The Captain briefly contemplated letting the Polyphase Avatron tear Mr Fibuli apart, but settled for a hissed 'Speak!'

'The Mentiads are marching on the city, sir!' Mr Fibuli explained.

This could mean only one thing. Somewhere in the city another telepath had been born, and they meant to take him.

'Vultures of death! Ghouls!' The Captain was on his feet, scrolling through the surveillance feeds until he found a group of pale figures in cloaks approaching the outskirts of the city. 'They're heading towards Sector Five. The telepath must not be taken.' He leaned into a microphone and barked out orders to the nearest Guards. 'Find him and destroy him! Or by all the suns that blaze, I'll tear you apart, molecule from molecule.'

On the screens, the Mentiads' progress was blocked by a group of Guards. Without warning, they raised their guns and fired on the Mentiads. The Captain hissed with delight – but the energy bolts failed to connect. The Mentiads simply stared at the Guards, their pale faces tight with concentration. The bolts fizzled away. One Guard rushed forward to try and use his gun as a club, but a Mentiad raised a slender, pale arm and sent the Guard flying into a wall.

Mr Fibuli took all this in. The Mentiads were stronger than he'd ever seen them before. He risked a nervous glance at the Captain and realised his pet was glaring hungrily at him.

'Idiots!' the Captain roared. 'All Guards, the Mentiads are heading towards Sector Six. Find the telepath before they do. Find him and destroy him!'

The Doctor had surveyed the living room and swiftly taken charge. The old man and the young girl were frantic with worry. The arrogant young man was afraid someone would tell him he didn't matter, and the ill young man was in need of help.

The Doctor was tending to Pralix while reassuring his sister Mula. 'So,' he was saying to her, 'your brother Pralix has fallen into a state of shock.'

'He does this every time the Captain announces a New Golden Age of Prosperity.'

That phrase again, the Doctor thought. 'He does this every time?'

'Well, the last two or three times, yes.'

'I see.' The Doctor didn't, but wasn't going to let that get in the way. 'And tell me about this Captain. Pleasant sort of chap, is he?'

Mula and her grandfather exchanged worried glances. Kimus was clearly working himself up for an angry outburst.

'We've never seen him,' explained Mula.

'But he is great and good. He looks after us and makes us rich.'

'Hah!' Here it came from Kimus. 'He makes us all his fools.'

'Really? That's a very interesting observation,' said the Doctor politely.

The comatose Pralix twisted and murmured in his fever. 'The Mentiads!' He suddenly sprang to life on the couch, twisting himself up. His eyes were wild and he looked terrified. 'The Mentiads! They are coming!' he shrieked.

Oh dear, thought the Doctor. That did not sound good.

Up on the Bridge, the Captain was coordinating the search, pulling information from the myriad of security screens faster than any of his crew could hope to. Even his Nurse was standing back and admiring his efficiency. 'Find the telepath!'

Suddenly the Captain came to a juddering halt, panting with exertion. The Nurse rushed to his side, but he pushed her away.

'What was that?' he groaned. Something had glided past one of the cameras. Barely in shot, little more than a shadow. But the Captain had not missed it. And neither had his pet. The Polyphase Avatron threw itself from the Captain's shoulder, its beak pecking furiously at the screen.

The Nurse blinked. Even she was surprised to find the Captain confused. She was not quite sure what effect this would have on his health.

'What the planet's bane is that?' demanded the Captain, his one eye boggling.

The Polyphase Avatron was hopping anxiously on his shoulder, screeching with rage. The screens of the Bridge were filled with the remarkable image of a small robot dog, gliding neatly into a house. 'Search that house!' the Captain thundered. 'That house! Search it and kill everything inside!'

K-9 entered the house with a gliding saunter, unaware that he'd just betrayed its occupants to the Captain. The humanoids reacted very favourably to his arrival: the Doctor-Master beamed, while the others expressed wonder and amazement.

'Captain save us!' wailed the ageing male.

'What is that thing?' asked the younger male.

'Is it a machine?' suggested the female.

And the clearly ill humanoid male emitted an involuntary psychic distress call on some fascinating frequencies. K-9 analysed them. Curious. But not the same interference he'd detected earlier. That was still out there: another robotic creature, vastly inferior.

'Don't worry.' The Doctor patted K-9 on the head. 'This is a friend of mine. Aren't you a friend of mine, K-9?'

'Affirmative, Master.' The dog risked waggling his tail. 'Friend.'

'So K-9, these people were telling me about the Mentiads. Who are they? Why are they coming here?'

'They are evil zombies! They have terrible powers,' the old man began ranting.

K-9 interrupted; he had an important mission of his own. 'Master,' he began. 'The Mistress is in danger.'

The Doctor didn't hear because the young man sat up on the couch, shaking. 'Danger!' he wailed. 'They're coming.'

'What do they want from you, Pralix?' the Doctor asked.

Which was when some of the Captain's Guards entered the house, kicking open the door, smashing their way through the chairs, and aiming their weapons at the cowering group.

So K-9 stunned them one after the other. Now, perhaps, the Doctor would let him explain about the Mistress Romana before the Guards recovered.

The Doctor-Master grinned with pleasure, clearly dismissing the Guards. 'Evil zombies, terrible powers? Pah.'

'Those were not the Mentiads,' said the humanoid female. 'Those were the Captain's Guards.'

This didn't please the Doctor-Master.

'The Mentiads!' shrieked the ill young man on the couch.

The old man seemed in even greater distress. 'We must hide him. They must be nearly here. Oh, the Captain's way was better.'

The female approached this sensibly. 'There is nowhere we can hide him.'

The angry young male was calling everyone in the room cowards and demanding they fight. Although K-9 noted that, of them all, only he was equipped with offensive capability.

'Pralix, can you hear my voice?' The Doctor-Master stared into the ill young man's empty eyes with concern. 'Who are the Mentiads? Why do they want you?'

'We're not going to be pampered, frightened vegetables any more!' shouted the angry man, and then fell silent, backing away in terror as a group of new arrivals entered the room.

K-9 assessed them as roughly humanoid, malnourished, their bodies emitting an extraordinary amount of psychic energy.

Their appearance delighted the Doctor-Master. 'Hello! Hello! Are you by any chance the Mentiads?' He swept up to them and offered a hand to shake in humanoid greeting. 'You look like the Mentiads to me and—'

The new arrivals did not acknowledge him. Almost in passing, just for a moment, they glanced at the Doctor-Master, their eyes that little bit wider. A glow enveloped him, throwing him back against the wall. K-9 tried firing at them, but his blaster had no effect.

The Doctor-Master was still talking. 'You see, I was wondering if …' He tailed off and slumped to the floor, his mind suddenly and completely empty.

The Mentiads stepped over him, pushed the other humans aside, and stood over Pralix.

Chapter Four

Late to the Party

The Captain was working out who to kill.

He had lined his crew up on the Bridge and was marching up and down in front of them. The Polyphase Avatron was hopping excitedly on his shoulders as he stared each man in the eye. The Captain's Nurse stood to one side – not to help any of the victims, but in case he became overexcited.

'The rogue telepath has not been destroyed,' the Captain rumbled, low and dangerous. 'I ordered that he should be. Instead he has been allowed to fall into the hands of the Mentiads. I ordered that he should not be so allowed. Failure is something I find it very hard to come to terms with. Is that not so, Mr Fibuli?'

'Yes sir, that's very true, sir.' Mr Fibuli spoke from bitter experience.

'By all the flaming moons of hell, it is not two hours since you very nearly blew up every engine in this mountain!'

The engineer next to Mr Fibuli smirked. He even gave Mr Fibuli a wink. A wink that said, 'You're for it, mate.'

Somehow Mr Fibuli found his voice. 'Well, Captain, you said yourself the cause was external. Something extraordinary happened to the whole fabric of the space-time continuum at that moment.' He then risked a look back at the engineer.

'Have you discovered the cause of that yet?'

'Not yet, sir. Busy working on it, sir,' Fibuli admitted miserably.

'Then you have failed to find it, Mr Fibuli.' The Captain leaned over, his hot, diesel breath wafting over Mr Fibuli's face.

Out of the corner of his eye, Mr Fibuli saw the engineer risk a sarcastic wave.

The Captain stepped back, turning to his pet. 'Failed, failed, failed!' he clucked. 'And, my sweet, when someone fails me, someone dies!'

The parrot nodded, spread its wings, and soared up, eyes glowing at the thought of a kill.

Mr Fibuli shut his eyes. He didn't want to see it coming. He really didn't.

He felt the brush of wind as the parrot swooped down.

There was a blast and a terrible scream of agony.

Mr Fibuli realised that the scream wasn't coming from him.

He opened his eyes.

The Avatron was pecking at the smouldering remains of the engineer who had been standing next to him.

The Captain tapped the side of his nose with a clang.

'I hope you find the cause very soon, Mr Fibuli. I hope you will not fail me again.'

'Doctor?'

'Shush.'

'Doctor!' It was Mula.

The Doctor woke up reluctantly and found himself on a couch being stared at by Kimus, Mula and Balaton. He felt utterly spent and just for once in his life wanted no part in whatever their problems were. He just wanted a blanket, some dolly mixtures, and a quiz show.

K-9 was extending a probe to his forehead.

'What hit me?' groaned the Doctor.

Kimus spoke. 'It was the Mentiads. I don't know what they used to hit—'

'I'm not asking you,' the Doctor dismissed him. 'K-9, what hit me?'

'According to my instruments, Master, it was a gestalt-generated psychokinetic blast on a wavelength of 338.79 micropars reaching a peak power level of 5347.2 on the Vantalla Psychoscale.'

'5347.2? Yes, that's exactly what it felt like,' the Doctor said ruefully, making an effort to sit up. Pure mental energy. No wonder he felt glum. Still, give him ten minutes of peace and he'd be back to top billing.

'Pralix is gone! What is to be done?' wailed Balaton. 'The Mentiads have taken him!'

'Don't worry, I'll find him.' The Doctor wobbled to his feet and regretted his life choices.

'That is if he's still alive,' Kimus sneered.

Mula's face crumpled, and the Doctor knew how she felt. 'You're very well informed,' he said to Kimus. 'Perhaps you can tell me where they've taken him?'

That stumped Kimus. 'They just arrive in the city and then depart. They're all too scared to follow them.'

'They?'

'Cowards,' pronounced Kimus. 'The other people who live in this city.'

'Not you, though? You're not frightened?'

'No.' Kimus beat his chest.

'You just didn't get round to it, is that it?'

The wind went out of Kimus's sails. 'I will follow them – of course—'

'Splendid idea!' the Doctor agreed. 'Let's go together.'

'Now?' The smile vanished from Kimus's face. Good. The Doctor cheered up. A plan was forming and things were going his way. Only K-9 interrupted.

'Master?'

'Not now, K-9. Can you track the Mentiads by their psychospore?'

'Affirmative, Master. However—' The dog wanted to talk about something else. Best put a stop to that.

'Excellent. Right, who's coming with us? Mula? Balaton?'

Balaton started to wail with misery, so that left him out.

'What about Romana? She'll come.' A thought struck him. 'Where's Romana?'

'She has been arrested, Master.' What? 'She sent me to inform you.'

'Why didn't you?'

A gentle electronic cough. 'I made four attempts, Master, but you would not allow me to tell you.'

Oh. The Doctor caught Kimus smirking and decided not to let this set him back. 'Well then – it just means two rescue attempts!' Romana was new, she hadn't even got her badge for Being Captured. Plus she had the Tracer and there was every danger that by the time he'd caught up with her she'd have found the next segment and that would never do. 'Where will they have taken her?'

'To the Captain.' Mula's voice had the sympathetic edge of one breaking bad news. 'On the mountain.'

'No one ever comes back from seeing the Captain.' Kimus was now outdoing Balaton in passing on bad news.

'No one?' the Doctor asked, practically rubbing his hands with glee.

'No one. Except the Guards,' said Mula and shook her head sadly. 'Your friend, Doctor, is already dead.'

*

49

The Guard dragged Romana into a small square in the city. The citizens there drew back, not meeting her eye, which Romana considered a little rude. The Guard threw her towards what could only be an air-car – a quaint little plastic bubble resting on two anti-gravity skis. 'Get in,' he growled.

'I shall take that as an invitation.' Romana gave him her very sincerest smile. The Guard found himself handing her into the air-car. 'Thank you,' she said, sitting down at the controls, and patted the seat next to her. 'Will you drive? I could … but I assume you know where we're going.'

Meanwhile, the Doctor was attempting to explain the key project management tool of tossing a coin. His audience was not promising – apart from Mula who clearly did all the work around here. There was Balaton who'd spent a lifetime sighing and Kimus who'd spent his saying how much better things could be if only someone did something.

'Heads we go after Romana first, tails we go after Pralix first.'

The Doctor threw the coin. Mula examined it. It had landed heads up.

'How can you take such a dangerous decision like that, just leaving it to chance?' she asked.

'Ah,' the Doctor confided in her, sheepishly. 'It's a two-headed coin, see? There are two kings on Aldebaran Three.'

'That's not fair,' said Mula. She was also wondering what or where was Aldebaran Three. 'I'm going after Pralix.'

'But Mula—' the Doctor began.

She pushed past him. 'He's my brother. I'll find my own way!' And with that she went out into the street. The Doctor decided he liked her.

Kimus laid a not entirely welcome hand on the Doctor's shoulder. 'No use once she's made up her mind.' A short, cunning pause. 'I'll go after her.' Clearly he'd seized on a way to avoid going to meet the Captain.

The Doctor seized it back. 'No, no, Kimus, you're coming with me,' he insisted. 'K-9, you take Mula to find the Mentiads. My new friend and I will go rescue Romana.'

Romana was finding the ride in the air-car charmingly quaint.

'Ah.' She dug her Guard in the ribs. 'I had an air-car rather like this once. It was a present for my 70th birthday.' She ran a critical eye over the controls while adjusting her hair. 'Do you know that if you realign the magnetic vector and fit a polarity oscillator you get twice the speed for half the energy?'

The Guard blinked. Normally by this point in their journey to the Captain his prisoners were pleading, babbling in hysterics, or throwing themselves out of the air-car to their doom. The Guard wondered what the Captain would make of his prisoner.

Hopefully something agonising.

The Doctor had decided to take Kimus under his wing. If the young man wanted to be a rebel, then he was going to show him how. Kimus hadn't quite given up on talking the Doctor out of actually doing anything, though. He pointed out the top of the mountain.

'The Captain lives up there – on the Bridge.'

'And how do we get to it?'

'We don't,' Kimus said firmly.

'Like that, is it?' The Doctor had encountered this kind of situation before. Normally some solution or other presented itself.

They entered a square. At the end of it was an ornately decorated air-car.

'What about one of those?' the Doctor said hopefully.

Kimus looked shocked. The air-cars were only for the use of the Guards. Or their prisoners – and they only got one trip.

'Help me borrow it,' the Doctor grinned wickedly.

'Borrow it?'

'Sometimes it's nice to go first class, don't you think?'

The Doctor strolled across the square, then noticed a Guard leaning against the air-car, and ducked behind a pillar. Kimus joined him, hoping he'd see sense. The Doctor reached into his pocket and threw a small paper bag at the car. It landed on the bonnet, scattering an assortment of brightly coloured objects.

The Guard snapped into alertness, picking up and examining the objects. He was used to seeing gemstones everywhere, but these were different. Brightly coloured. Squishy. He followed a trail into the shadows by a pillar.

'Are those bombs?' Kimus whispered in awe as the Doctor dragged him stealthily into the air-car.

'No,' the Doctor confessed. 'Liquorice allsorts.'

The Guard didn't notice the thieves until it was too late. The air-car shot straight up into the air, wobbled, and then soared towards the mountain. The Doctor leaned out and waved at him.

'Bye-bye!'

Mr Fibuli had decided that the best way to break bad news was at a run. He dashed into the Bridge and tried getting the Captain's attention with a nervous simper.

The Captain was having his temperature taken by his nurse, and both of them turned to look at him sourly.

'More bad news?' the Nurse asked perceptively, and Mr Fibuli remembered why he'd never cared for her.

'Well ...'

'By the horns of the prophet Balag, speak!' the Captain roared.

The Nurse anxiously adjusted a control on her medical pack, and some of the colour went out of the old pirate's face.

The words poured out of Mr Fibuli. Because this was very bad news indeed and his legs were urging him to keep running and never stop. 'The Macromat Field Integrator has burnt out, sir. It's one of the four components we can't replace ourselves. We are faced with two alternatives, Captain. Three alternatives. We can try to find a new Macromat Field Integrator, though I can't envisage how we would do that ...'

The colour had returned to the Captain's face. He waved the Nurse away, staggered out of his chair and loomed over Mr Fibuli, hissing at him.

Somehow, the ship's mate continued. 'So, alternatively, there is a very rare mineral, PJX18, which would conceivably do the same job as the integrator, if we could find any of it, that is ...'

The Captain drew a rattling breath. The Nurse tutted, and reached for her blood pressure monitor.

'In our current condition we could only possibly make one more jump and that would be risky in the extreme, sir.'

The Captain started to let out all that breath he'd taken in. 'And the third alternative?'

'Well ...' Mr Fibuli risked a glance at the view from the dome. The two suns were reasonable, the skyline nice enough. Maybe he'd go for it? 'The other option is for Zanak to settle where it is, sir.'

'Forever?'

'Yes sir.'

'I see.' The Captain considered this news silently, then chopped his arm onto a control panel, shattering it in two. Sparks landed on his face as he bellowed: 'No, by the Sky Demon! I say no!'

'I'm afraid –' Mr Fibuli squeezed a very tiny last bit of courage out of the tube – 'that that's it, unless another option presents itself, sir.'

Which was when Romana was brought in.

'Hey, this is marvellous!' Kimus was enjoying the ride in the air-car.

The one dog-like thing that K-9 never did was stick his head out the window. The Doctor thought that was a shame.

'This is freedom at last!' Kimus cried, his head swaying, leaning over from one side of the air-car to the other, chewing happily away on the last few sweets from the Doctor's pockets. His feeling of independence was probably mixed with a sugar rush.

The Doctor found it all rather distracting while he was trying to steer. 'You're not free yet, not by a long way.'

'Free to think!' Kimus wriggled himself over the windshield, leaning over to look at the city beneath them. He turned back to the Doctor, desperate for approval. 'It's amazing. The city looks so pretty from up here. Yes, even the mines do. You know, that's our entire life down there.'

'These mines –' the Doctor picked the word that had interested him – 'tell me about them.'

'Well, we extract all the raw material we need from the mines. It's terribly efficient.'

'Who goes down them? Do you?' He tried to imagine Kimus doing an honest day's toil when someone else could do it for him.

'Me, no!' Kimus confirmed the Doctor's impression.

'The Mentiads?' That was an intriguing possibility. Psychic power achieved by exposure to whatever was in the mines.

'Them? No chance. It's all automated, we just run the equipment.'

'And what happens when the mines run empty?'

'Oh well ...' Kimus shrugged. 'The Captain just announces a new Golden Age of Prosperity, and they fill up again.'

The Doctor nearly plunged the air-car into a tailspin.

'Whee!' exclaimed Kimus.

'They fill up?' The Doctor spoke slowly. 'Just like that?'

'Well yes.' Kimus frowned. 'You don't think that's wrong do you?'

'Wrong? It's an economic miracle. Of course it's wrong.'

'Oh, and then, of course, the lights change,' muttered Kimus dreamily.

'What lights?' The Doctor's hand gripped the steering wheel tightly.

'Oh, you know. The omens.' Kimus frowned, baffled. He pointed up. 'The ones in the sky at night, the little points of light.'

'Do you mean the stars?'

'Stars, eh? Is that what you call them? Fancy,' Kimus continued. 'Yes, they keep putting up new ones. Seems pointless to me but the old people do seem to like it.'

'Do they indeed?' sighed the Doctor. His mind was connecting the dots and not liking the picture one bit.

'Look down there!' Kimus was distracted by the view again. 'There's some sort of entrance into the mountain!'

'Might get us to the Captain.' The Doctor, without even seeming to notice, angled the air-car into a smooth dive.

'Hey, you're very good at that.' Kimus bounced in his seat. 'Do you drive these things for a living?'

'No,' the Doctor was grim. 'I save planets mostly. But this time I think I've arrived far, far too late.'

Chapter Five

The Normally Delicious Smell of Pork

Romana's first impression was that the Captain was something a madman might have made – given a pile of body parts, half an hour, and an old washing machine, he'd have pulled back a dust cloth and with a cheery 'ta-da!' unveiled the figure before her.

The creature looked absolutely disgusting and terribly pathetic. Whoever had done this had clearly not given a hoot about what the Captain felt. He must be mad with pain.

The Captain strode towards her, metallic joints squeaking, servos tearing, the air filling with the smell of a Sunday roast left too long in an oven.

Romana prepared to tell him her name and that she'd just graduated from the Time Lord Academy with a Triple First. Once that had won him over, she'd explain politely that she was looking for the Key to Time, and that, after it had been handed over, she'd do something about the squeak in his left elbow and be on her way.

The Captain's metal eye glared at her. 'What is your function?'

Oh. Romana felt a little disappointed. This was her first interrogation, after all, and if they weren't even going to ask about her qualifications, then what was the point of it all? She was beginning to see why the Doctor couldn't take these types entirely seriously. I mean, clearly, they were capable of doing terrible things and causing immense cruelty, but all the shouting, dear me.

It was then that Romana noticed the silly robot bird perched on the Captain's shoulder, scowling at her. Romana paid it not the slightest bit of attention. She had thinking to do.

'My function?' she tried to be polite. 'Well, as a Time Lord, I can travel about in space and, of course—'

The brute cut her off for more ranting. 'Pah! A common space urchin. You shall die.'

The problem with the Captain, Romana posited, was that he was both literally and figuratively lacking in gears. She examined a nail. The cuticle was looking a trifle ragged. 'I travel in space,' she repeated slowly, 'and, of course, time. Hence Time Lord.' She beamed at the Captain, encouragingly.

'Time travel?' The Captain gave a tin sneer. 'Time travel? You expect me to believe such nonsense?'

Romana clucked with sympathy. 'Yes, it is a difficult concept, isn't it?'

Had he been watching and scoring proceedings, the Doctor would have applauded while being worried that she'd overplayed her serve.

The Captain tottered towards her with badly oiled fury. 'The insolent breath of idle fantasy! Death Comes Now!'

The robot parrot launched itself from the Captain's shoulder, incinerated a nearby chair for the sake of intimidation and then dived towards Romana, squawking. Romana decided it was hard to be dignified when you were about to be executed by a robot parrot.

The Captain's Nurse appeared on the Bridge, smoothing down her pale green uniform. Romana regarded the new arrival with some surprise. The starched clothes, the meek attitude, all seemed strangely out of place, and yet very welcome. How nice to find the Citadel wasn't just full of shouting men.

The Nurse spoke gently, but with authority. 'Captain,' she said in very soothing tones. 'The excitement of more than one execution in a day is bad for your blood pressure. Perhaps you should consider postponing it till tomorrow.'

'Postpone?' The Captain's voice was that of a sulky child sent to bed without any supper.

'I really do think it best,' the Nurse purred. She gestured, and the robot bird fluttered back to its perch on the Captain's shoulder. 'Besides –' the Nurse favoured Romana with a surprisingly charming smile –

'I think her story sounds quite fascinating even if it is idle fantasy. Why don't you ask her how this machine she mentioned travels?'

'Speak!' the Captain snapped, trying to regain the situation.

Ah well, Romana thought, let's see. 'Roughly speaking, and putting it terribly simply, the TARDIS dematerialises in this dimension, passes through a space-time vortex and then rematerialises again in a new location.'

She waited for her words to sink in. The drive technicians were staring at her. A fussy man with a clipboard was gaping. The Captain appeared to be trying to frown.

'Well now ...' The Nurse's voice came floating through the stunned silence. 'I think that sounds jolly interesting. Don't you?'

I seem to have made quite the impression, thought Romana. But why?

The air-car had landed a long way up the mountain on a smooth plateau dotted with snow. Far beneath them lay the desert and the shimmering city. Ahead of them was a door, painted the same dark grey as the rock.

Kimus tried the door. It was locked. 'We'll never get it open. It's impossible.'

'Impossible? Oh dear.' The Doctor's face fell. 'That means it's probably going to take at least 73 seconds,

73 seconds which we can ill afford.' He moved Kimus out of the way and gave the door a very hard stare.

Kimus was worried. He had hoped this would be the end of this adventure. 'You mean you can open it?'

'Well, of course I can open it. It's just a question of how.'

'But how?'

'I haven't got the faintest idea.' He took out his trusty sonic screwdriver, which had opened everything from a tyrant's dungeon to a village fête. Nothing happened.

'Nothing happened!' exclaimed Kimus, with unnecessary relief.

'I've not finished yet.' The Doctor dug about in his pockets and pulled out a small bit of metal. 'Bent hairpin,' he announced and plunged it into the door. 'People often overlook the obvious.' With a click, the door slid back into the rock face.

Kimus stared at him with amazement. 'How did you do that?'

The Doctor shrugged. 'The more sophisticated the technology, the more vulnerable it is to primitive attack. Shall we go in?'

Kimus wanted nothing more than to run away, but the Doctor had already stepped inside. With little choice, Kimus trotted glumly after him into the mountain.

*

Up on the Bridge, the Captain had had the worried-looking man bring over a large burned cube of metal for Romana to look at.

'Is this some kind of test?' she'd asked. The Captain had laughed. Several of the crew had laughed. The worried man had given her a sympathetic look. Romana peered at the object dubiously. 'Well, whatever it is, it's obviously burnt to a crisp.'

'Ha!' the Captain chortled. 'A whining infant could tell me that. Your time is running out.' He gestured to his robot parrot, hopping impatiently from claw to claw, singeing the air.

Romana was thoroughly bored of both of them. 'I'm sorry,' she yawned. 'I was never any good at antiques.'

'Antiques?' the Captain yelped, his voice embarrassingly high. The Nurse hurried anxiously to his side.

'Yes.' Romana poked the melted tangle with a fingertip. 'I mean, it's probably just an old Macromat Field Integrator or something.'

Every eye on the Bridge was trained on her, every breath held. Goodness me, I am having quite the effect on the locals, Romana thought.

'Captain, she *does* know what it is,' whispered the worried man.

The Nurse gave Romana a quick, friendly glance of approval.

The Captain dragged himself over to her, and landed an arm on her shoulder. Romana wasn't sure if it was a friendly gesture or a half-hearted mugging, but she kept her feet and smiled broadly at him.

'By the beard of the Sky Demon, the jaws of death were hot about your neck, girl,' the Captain confided. He sounded impressed. So Romana risked another deduction.

'If it is, then it must be part of a massive dematerialisation circuit.'

The Captain nodded, and there was an entirely new tone in his voice – no, wait, something was lacking. He wasn't shouting at her. Nor was he sneering. Instead he was – with as much of his lip as he had – smiling. 'It is part of a system that transports us instantly through space.'

'The whole mountain?' Romana did some frantic blinking. Quite beyond why you would do something like that, as an achievement it was impressive. 'You take this whole mountain with you through space?'

Much to her surprise, the Captain burst out laughing. As did the crew.

The Doctor and Kimus were confronted by an endless corridor going into the mountain.

'A corridor!' exclaimed Kimus. 'It must go on for ever.'

'Yes it certainly looks like it.' The Doctor really couldn't get worked up about an abundance of corridor. Especially one that went on in a long straight line with no doors.

Kimus found some heroism and plunged off down the corridor, running very fast.

The Doctor watched for a while, pulling a paper bag from his pocket, unwrapping and then sucking slowly on a boiled sweet.

Kimus was running very fast and going nowhere. His feet kept moving, but completely failed to gain any friction on the surface. He was, in effect, running on the spot, or at least a couple of microns above it.

Realising that something was wrong, Kimus looked at his pedalling feet and then back at the Doctor. 'Hey, what's happening? This floor doesn't work.'

The Doctor reached out and pulled Kimus out of the corridor. Kimus stood, panting at the edge of it, perplexed.

'Kimus, I want you to do something very important for me.'

Kimus, distracted by the seriousness of the Doctor's tone, nodded glumly.

'Go out to the air-car, there's a gun in the glove compartment. Stand outside on guard.'

Kimus's face fell. If they were inside the mountain then maybe they stood a chance of success, in which case perhaps there'd be some heroism to be had.

'Doctor, I'd rather come with you.'

'No.' The Doctor shook his head gravely. 'Standing watch is the most valuable thing you can do. There are so many things here you can't understand, and a linear induction corridor is one of them.' He reached up to a panel on the wall, slipped it open, and turned the corridor on. 'Watch this,' he said, and stepped into the corridor.

Kimus watched in amazement as the Doctor was whisked away from him at a remarkable speed. He darted after him but nothing happened. He jabbed at the button but, again, nothing happened. The Doctor had by now receded to a distant point of light that was waving vaguely.

The linear induction corridor was really very, very efficient. 'Fascinating,' the Doctor wobbled. 'Hmmm, it is actually terribly fast. I think I'd better have another humbug, just to steady my nerves.'

He was starting to feel rather giddy.

Much to his distress, the Doctor accelerated again, pinging towards a wall. He cried out in alarm, only to find himself swerved sickeningly around a previously hidden corner.

The Doctor zoomed on towards the heart of the mountain.

While logic was telling him that all would be well with the corridor, his every instinct was telling him to curl up into a ball and howl. The Doctor had abandoned his earlier sangfroid for a rather less dignified crouch, his hands thrown over his face.

As the walls whipped past at a blur, he made a solemn vow: 'I'll never be cruel to an electron in a particle accelerator again!'

The corridor took another dizzying, sickening, Planck-irritating turn, and a very solid wall loomed up ahead. He was now very alarmed, and science wasn't helping. At this speed, and without a very large and comfy net at the end, he was going to end up as a bohemian chutney.

With an abrupt yet subtle halt, the Doctor stopped moving. He was simply standing at the end of the corridor, its quiet hum gently mocking him. He peeped out from between his fingers, finding his nose millimetres from a wall.

He found some breath, patted himself gently all over, just to make sure he was still all there. 'Ah! Of course, not a linear induction corridor, it must work by neutralising inertia.'

A steel shutter slammed down behind him.

'Ah. More sudden death, I expect.' The Doctor was starting to calculate his escape options when he spotted the control panel on the steel shutter. 'Oh, I beg your pardon – you're a lift!'

Meanwhile, Romana was re-examining the ruins of the Macromat Field Integrator. The worried little man (who seemed to be called Mr Fibuli, of all things) was most insistent that perhaps she might be able to do something.

'Well, yes, I could throw it away,' she'd retorted. That had not gone down well.

The Captain had hissed menacingly, his tin bird had glowered, and even the Nurse had tutted. Mr Fibuli had simply looked wretched. So Romana had picked up the wrecked component and given it a polite squint.

'Do you think she can repair it, Mr Fibuli?' the Captain hissed curiously.

'Well, in my opinion it's irreparable,' Mr Fibuli whispered. 'But it occurs to me, Captain, that she must have something similar aboard her own vessel, and perhaps we should …'

The Captain's rare and unusual smile widened, showing off a row of metal teeth. He strode over to Romana. 'Girl! What is your diagnosis? Can it be repaired?'

'Repaired? Oh yes, I should think so,' Romana offered.

'Then do so! Now! Instantly!' the Captain roared.

Every urge she had to help expired then and there. She had an idea. 'But you'd have to ask the Doctor.'

'Doctor?' the Captain rumbled. 'Are there further intruders upon this planet?'

'Oh yes.' Romana checked the Doctor wasn't within hearing range, and then bubbled. 'You see, I'm only his assistant. He's the one you should be talking to. Or rather listening to, that is, if you have the stamina.'

Excited, the Captain snatched up a microphone and began barking orders into it. 'All Guards on alert! There is an intruder on Zanak, he must be found! His name is the Doctor, repeat the Doctor, he must be found and brought to the Bridge instantly!'

The main door to the Bridge opened, and the Doctor strode in.

That, thought Romana, will do nicely.

Chapter Six

Dark Satanic Mills

A squadron of the Captain's Guards rushed past the Doctor without noticing him. He'd had quite enough of this planet ignoring him. He grabbed a Guard by the hand and shook it.

'Hello! I'm the Doctor.'

The Guard stopped, blinked, and rushed on. Snubbed, the Doctor marched further onto the Bridge, took it all in, and smiled. This was decidedly more like it. A crazed cyborg, a group of terrorised technicians, a frightened henchman, a nurse (*mental note: try to win her over in case things go wrong and you find yourself being locked up and/or sacrificed*), Romana looking at her most Romana, and joy of joys, a robot parrot. Home ground at last.

'Who are you?' demanded the swaggering cyborg.

'Hello, hello, I'm the Doctor!' He cut the Captain completely and turned his full charm on Mr Fibuli, grabbing his hand and pumping it enthusiastically. 'I'm the Doctor. Delighted to meet you. Heard so much about what a splendid chap you are. I see you've met my assistant, Romana. Getting on like a house on fire, are you? She's a lovely girl.' He gave her a cheery wave. 'What a splendid place you've got here. Are you having a spot of bother?'

'Seize him!' thundered the Captain.

'Such hospitality,' the Doctor grinned. 'I'm underwhelmed.'

He happily let himself be seized. You can tell a lot about an adversary by the quality of their seizing.

The Captain was used to having things go his way, and he was not sure he was enjoying today. He strode over to the Doctor for a bit of towering and glaring. 'Doctor, your manner appeals only to the homicidal side of my nature.'

'My manners are impeccable.' The Doctor beamed and made a little chirruping noise, jerking his nose towards the Polyphase Avatron.

Romana had never seen a robot parrot roll its eyes before.

With barely an effort, the Doctor shrugged himself free of the Guards and strolled over to Romana.

She handed him the remains of the component. 'I think this is the root of the trouble, Doctor.'

The Doctor sucked air professionally through his teeth. 'Was that a Macromat Field Integrator? Whizzbang gone wrong?'

'Yes.' Romana was a little impressed. 'And the Ambicyclic Photon Bridge is fused.'

The Doctor sniffed. '*And* the Ambicyclic Photon Bridge? Tut tut.'

'Quite.' Romana clucked with mock sympathy, and, just for a moment, the two Time Lords looked each other in the eye and grinned. It was, Romana thought, good to have the Doctor here.

'I wonder if I could examine it in situ?' the Doctor ventured. 'It would help me diagnose what went wrong.'

'Nothing went wrong!' the Captain roared. 'And you shall not see my engines!'

'Apparently they're quite impressive,' said Romana in a stage whisper.

'*Quite*?' the Captain boiled.

Mr Fibuli looked at the Captain beseechingly.

The Captain, remembering Plan B, capitulated. 'Take them to the Engine Room. If they make a single mistake, kill them.'

'Gosh,' said the Doctor as they were led away.

At the door, Romana turned, 'Oh, Mr Fibuli?'

'Yes?'

She tossed the remains of the Macromat Field Integrator at him. He failed to catch them, and they shattered on the floor.

The entire mountain was hollow and mostly engine. Pistons the height of tower blocks surged up and down, heat blazed from dozens of outlet vents, and the air was full of shouts and calls from the crew as countless systems were engaged. The sheer scale of the endeavour was staggering.

'Whoa! Look at it all, Romana!' The Doctor was behaving with the gusto of an excited tourist seeing their first service station.

'Amazing.' And Romana meant it. 'I suppose you're going to tell me you've seen it all before.'

'No, actually. Not like this.' The Doctor's grin was going nowhere near his eyes. He stroked and prodded gargantuan levers, emitting a series of hisses and gasps, a schoolboy doing impressions of a steam train. 'I suspected something of the kind, of course.'

Standing on a distant gantry the Captain were watching them. Even from this distance, they could discern Mr Fibuli fidgeting nervously at his side. The Polyphase Avatron flitted between the massive silos.

The Doctor stepped back and gave them all a cheery wave. 'Let's look busy,' he told Romana through gritted teeth. He sauntered over to a row of glowing glass valves. 'Magnificent. Well I never,' he cooed.

'What do you mean, you suspected something of the kind—'

'Shsssush!' hissed the Doctor. 'Look at this.' He was absorbed in the readings from a control panel. 'What do you make of this lot?'

'Well ...' Romana squinted.

'Gravitic Anomaliser input reading, nine point five!' the Doctor bellowed. 'Nine point five,' he repeated in a whisper. 'What does that mean?'

'Gravitic Anomaliser input reading nine point five, check,' Romana confirmed equally loudly, nodding seriously. She lowered her voice. 'You're saying you knew these engines were here. And that you already knew this mountain's really a spaceship and it's broken down?'

'The mountain?' The Doctor blinked. Was that really what she thought? Ah well. 'Less or more, yes.'

'But how? How did you know? What does this mountain have to do with the displacement of Calufrax?'

'Well …' The Doctor pulled a spanner from his pockets and, with it, turned the valves reverently. 'Let's just say, I just put 1.795372 and 2.204628 together, that's all.'

'What does that mean?'

'Four!' the Doctor cried, tossing the spanner into a corner.

Mr Fibuli was wondering what the strangers were doing here. The Guards had reported that they had located the strangers' craft, but had been unable to get into it.

The Captain shrugged, mildly annoying the Nurse who was trying to take his blood pressure. 'We must find out why there are here,' he growled. 'And we must allow them a little rope, so that they lead us into their vessel.'

'Does that include letting them discover the secret of Zanak's engines?' Mr Fibuli asked.

The Captain did not reply.

The Doctor examined an Ayres Silencer critically. 'We are in very great danger …'

'From the Captain?' Romana snorted. She'd been tutored by worse. 'He's just a terrible old bully. All that *By the evil nose of the Sky Demon* stuff. It's bluster.'

'The Captain is a very clever, very dangerous man, and he's just playing with us.'

'Why?'

The Doctor looked around at the vast engines, at the remorseless, perpetual motion of a vast machine setting itself against the universe.

'He's very keen to know what we know and why we're here.'

'The reason why we've come here is to find the second segment of the Key to Time, in case you've forgotten.' Romana slipped the Tracer quietly from her jacket and waved it around as though scanning a computer. How odd. 'Getting involved in all this is a bit of a sideshow.'

'It's the way to find the segment.' The Doctor tightened a screw. 'What does the Tracer say?'

Romana stared at the Tracer and shook it gently. It fizzed. She waved it subtly over the engines as though

76

inspecting them. Surprisingly the Tracer continued to fizz. 'I just don't understand it. If Calufrax has been displaced somehow, then why are we still detecting the segment? The Tracer gives out a continuous signal wherever we go.'

'What?' The Doctor listened to the gentle fizzing from the Tracer and frowned. 'That's it, then.'

'What?'

'The answer.' Ashen, the Doctor jammed his hands deep in his pockets and walked away from the engines. 'Romana, if I'm right we have stumbled on one of the most heinous crimes ever committed in this galaxy. We've got to get away from here and get away quickly.'

As he strode up to the gantry, the walls of the engines seemed to press in around him. The Doctor resisted the urge to gasp at what had had been done here. Instead he lifted a hand and waved it at Mr Fibuli.

'Hello! I think we've got to the root of the problem here,' the Doctor called up to them.

To Mr Fibuli's surprise, the Captain snapped back to life. He could have sworn the Captain hadn't breathed for minutes. 'Speak!'

'Your Magnifactoid Eccentricolometer's definitely on the blink,' the Doctor called.

'Is it really?' The Captain's hiss was louder than most men's screams. 'You know what will happen if I even begin to suspect you of sabotage?'

'Sabotage?' The Doctor looked hurt. 'Captain, that's more than my reputation's worth.'

The Captain snapped his fingers, and the Polyphase Avatron swooped low over the Doctor and Romana, causing them to duck.

'Or your life?' the Captain called.

'Or my life, as you say,' the Doctor agreed. 'We've got to go back to our own ship now and prepare some special equipment. Haven't we, Romana?'

'Oh yes, very special,' Romana agreed.

The two turned and headed straight for the exit.

'A moment!' the Captain called. 'The girl stays here.'

'The girl?' mouthed Romana, outraged.

The Doctor half-turned to the Captain. 'Now, I'm afraid that's not possible.' His tone perfectly conveyed how much he'd be only too happy to leave Romana behind. 'You see, we have a special lock on the TARDIS door.'

'We do?' This was outrageous news to Romana and sounded like a fib.

The Doctor winked at Romana. Romana, who had never winked before, winked back. It looked like something was in her eye.

'It needs the physical presence of us both to open it.' For just a moment the casual amiability dropped. 'Rather clever, don't you think?'

'Ah,' breathed Romana.

The Doctor waited.

The Captain snapped a tin finger and two Guards rushed to the time travellers' sides.

'Guards, escort them to their ship. Any attempt to escape is to be met with instant obliteration.'

The Doctor bowed low. 'Such a pleasure to work with you, Captain.' Then he turned to his Guards and beamed. 'Well, come on. Don't just stand there, escort us.'

Kimus was becoming bored. Was this really what being a rebel was like? So far he'd stood around for what felt like hours. He practised shooting some of the scrubby bushes dotted around the plateau. He'd thought about having a nap. It had started to rain gently.

In the end, his eyes drifted closed. Which meant that Kimus missed the arrival of a squad of Guards from the slopes above them. The Captain had thought about everything – the visitors were to have no outside help.

The first few shots missed Kimus, startling him awake. With the speed of a frightened rabbit, Kimus ran for the cover of the doorway. The Guards ran in pursuit, blasting away.

The Doctor smiled at Romana and tried to make small talk with their escorts, none of which was easy when hurtling down an inertia-free corridor. 'Standing around all day, looking tough. Must be very trying on the nerves?'

The Guards ignored the Doctor, faces impassive behind their masks. So the Doctor rapped one on the helmet and repeated his question.

Again, no answer.

'You're quite right,' the Doctor continued as though he had. 'Long hours, the violence, no intellectual stimulation.'

They reached the end of the corridor, and the Doctor stepped off with a queasy gasp.

'Are you all right?' he asked, helping Romana down.

'Perfectly, thank you,' she told him.

Which was when Kimus ran into them, pursued by a hail of blasts. The Doctor grabbed Kimus and dragged him and Romana to the floor – just as the two Guards behind them fired. So too did the Guards running after Kimus.

For a few moments, the air crackled with electricity.

When the smoke cleared, there was a pile of bodies in the cave.

The Doctor stood up sadly, addressing the body of the Guard he'd spoken to earlier. 'And now this happens. I'd give it up, if I were you.'

The Doctor helped a shaken Kimus to rise. 'Romana, this is Kimus. He's got an air-car, which is useful as we've got some travelling to do.' He led them out to the plateau.

'Where are we going?' Kimus asked.

'To investigate your mysterious mines.'

Romana had already slid into the driving seat. 'I'll drive,' she announced, revving the engine.

Mula and K-9 had been travelling for a long time. K-9 had led them out of the city, into the deserts, and to an opening in a dune. This had widened out into a cave, which had led them into a series of tunnels, which ended at a door.

'We have reached the end of the psychospore,' K-9 announced. 'This is where the Doctor-Master needs us to be.'

'And is this where the Mentiads live?' Mula asked.

'Affirmative.' K-9 had long-ago deduced this was the only possibility.

Mula opened the door and they stepped into a large underground cavern, a space empty apart from a few simple candles and a tang of misery in the air.

Standing in the exact centre of the room, Mula looked around. 'Where are the Mentiads?'

'They are all around us,' K-9 reported.

And the Mentiads stepped out from the shadows.

The Captain had returned to the Bridge and he was not in a good mood. 'Escaped! They've escaped?' the Captain was roaring at his crew. 'Your incompetence beggars the imagination!'

The Nurse rushed forward, concerned at the greasy smell coming from his joints, but the Captain shoved her away. 'There will be blood for this. Teeth of the Devil, there will be blood!'

The mine workings were remarkably plain. Romana was not impressed. She'd seen a city of diamonds, a citadel of stone and steel, and vast engines of precious metals precisely engineered. The mines were merely functional and cold and very abandoned.

'The interior of the mines is fully automated,' Kimus was explaining as he led them through rusting gates. 'There is an ancient lift shaft, but nobody's used it in living memory.'

'Why not?' Romana asked.

'The penalty is death.'

'Of course it is.' The Doctor lit up with enthusiasm. 'I can see there wouldn't be much incentive.'

They found the lift, and the Doctor went to work on the controls, breathing life into them. Romana looked at the basic cage, which swung slightly over a vast dark pit.

'Are you proposing we travel in that?' she asked. Trust the Doctor to find a method of transport even less appealing than his ancient TARDIS.

'Yes,' he said, leading them into the cage. It shuddered and sank just a little under their weight. 'I think it'll work.'

'You think?'

'Let's see!' the Doctor grinned, punched a button, and plunged them into the heart of the mines …

Mr Fibuli looked up from a screen; finally, some good news. 'Captain, sir, I've found them.'

'About time.' The Captain rounded on him. He had been staring out of the glass dome, down at the surface of Zanak below. 'Where?'

'They're in the mineshaft.'

The Captain's face flushed red. 'The mineshaft?' Was there nothing these strangers did not know? 'Moons of madness!' He flicked a switch, speaking into a grille. 'Guard Captain – we have intruders in the mineshaft. By the breath of the Sky Demon, they must be found.'

He turned back to Mr Fibuli. 'It seems we must find a way of breaking into their vessel without their help. Because once our visitors have seen what lies at the bottom of the mineshaft, they must never leave alive …'

'Doctor? Where are we?' Romana peered out into the gloom. It was freezing.

The Doctor produced a torch and waved it around. There was a small jump down from the lift platform onto the ground below. 'We're about three miles beneath the surface of Zanak.' He jumped.

'Three miles?' Romana followed. Had the journey really been that long?

'Yes.' Kimus leapt after her, landing with a splash. The lift cable creaked sadly. They were in some kind of rocky chamber, vast and utterly desolate.

'But it's so cold.' Romana was puzzled. 'You'd think we'd be feeling a rise in temperature by now, some geothermal heat ...'

'Yes.' The Doctor spoke with the air of a man dropping a fairly big hint. 'And yet here we are, somewhere cold and wet and icy.'

Romana didn't get it.

'This entire planet's hollow,' he continued.

'Hollow?'

The Doctor was used to companions who repeated his words back to him, but he'd been expecting better from a Time Lady with a Triple First. 'Yes. Hollow!'

'Then what are we standing on?'

'Can't you work it out? Take a look. Go on, look.'

They walked on, over the sludgy ground beneath them.

'It's all beyond me, Doctor. I don't know where I am,' admitted Kimus. His feet were wet and he did not like it.

'Kimus,' said the Doctor with gentle savagery. 'You are no longer standing on your world.'

Romana ran her hand through the cold stream and then straightened, splashing over to the bank. Flattened blades of grass poked up through the snow. She stopped.

'This is frozen ground,' she gasped. 'It shouldn't be here. Cold and wet. I don't understand.'

'Where are we?' asked Kimus.

The Doctor reached over to him. 'Listen, Kimus, the reason the lights in your sky keep changing is because they don't.'

'They don't?'

'No. What happens is, your whole planet jumps through space.'

Romana's mind made a horrified leap. 'The Captain's engines!'

'Engines huge enough to dematerialise the entire planet, flip it halfway across the galaxy and rematerialise it round its chosen prey ...'

'It preys on other worlds!' Romana was appalled.

'Wraps itself around them like a huge fist.' The Doctor clapped his hands around one of Romana's. It was not a reassuring gesture. The light from the torch went out.

'This entire planet is a huge hollow mining machine. It mines other planets, extracts all the valuable minerals and leaves the rubble behind.'

He shone his torch again, playing it over the vaulted ceiling above them. The light petered out, only just illuminating the vast lattice of iron above them. The crust of Zanak was braced together, a huge ceiling.

Romana was, quite literally, looking up at the roof of the world. 'Then what we're standing on now is the planet we originally came looking for?' She stared around her.

'Cold, wet, icy Calufrax.' The Doctor's voice echoed through the emptiness. 'She's buried inside Zanak, the Pirate Planet, having all the goodness sucked out of her, by the Captain.'

Kimus pulled a pebble from the bed of the stream. 'You mean whole other worlds have died to make us rich?'

The Doctor nodded. 'Whole other worlds.'

'Some of them inhabited,' Romana whispered.

'Remember the Oolion stone I picked up in the street?' The Doctor took the rare gem from his pocket. 'From Bandraginus Five. I knew I'd heard the name. A hundred years ago it disappeared. Vanished without trace. A planet of a thousand million people. Captain fodder.' He dropped the gem into the river. 'I've seen enough,' he said and stormed back to the lift.

Left alone, Kimus's only light was the soft glow of the Oolion stone shimmering through the water. He looked down at it. Someone should say something, to mark this moment.

'Bandraginus Five. By every last breath in my body, you will be avenged,' vowed Kimus. He felt it was what a hero would say, but in truth his heart just wasn't in it.

Kimus heard a noise and looked up, horrified.

The Doctor was about to scramble up to the lift, but Romana paused. She took the Tracer from her pocket and switched it on. It began to roar, a rush of static echoing back off the distant walls of Zanak and the forlorn surface of Calufrax.

'The reading's going mad!' cried Romana, fighting to turn off the Tracer.

'As well it might,' sighed the Doctor.

'The Second Segment of the Key to Time must be down here somewhere.'

'Yes, I thought so,' sighed the Doctor.

Kimus came running. No doubt with even more good news.

'Doctor—' he began, and then the blast knocked him flat.

The Captain's Guards were running behind him, firing. Spotlights stabbed down at them. More Guards were standing in the ironwork above them, taking aim. Shots rang out. Steam rose from the waters of Calufrax. Splinters of rocks flew through the air.

'Kill them! Kill them all!'

The Doctor and Romana grabbed a dazed Kimus and pelted across the slippery, icy surface. There was a mining corridor ahead of them. If only they could make it. They slid and scrabbled over ice, their way lit by gunfire.

'Doctor,' called a voice from ahead.

The Doctor slithered to a halt and motioned Romana and Kimus to do the same.

Standing in front of them was a group of figures, each one wrapped in cloak like a shroud.

The Guards, only a few paces behind, were levelling their guns when they saw the figures. They stopped and gasped.

One of the figures came forward and threw back his cowl.

'Doctor, we have come for you.' It was Pralix, his features pale, his red-rimmed eyes dead. 'The Mentiads have come for you all.'

Chapter Seven

The Death of Calufrax

Romana considered her situation, and she did not consider it favourably. Standing inside a hollow planet; behind her, men with guns; in front of her, a group of menacing people in cloaks. She was realising that the main reason why the Doctor was unable to take the universe entirely seriously was that things like this just kept happening to him.

The Guards did not consider their situation. 'Kill them! Kill them all!' they cried as they sprayed blaster fire through the cavern.

And that would have been the end of that, only Pralix smiled slightly. And all the other Mentiads smiled slightly. And the deadly blasts vanished completely.

A shimmering wall of energy had shut out the Guards and their weapons.

'What's happened to you, Pralix?' demanded Kimus.

Pralix smiled a little more, and Kimus didn't enjoy the smile.

'Hurry. Our force wall will not last long. We must go.' Pralix gestured to a tunnel behind them.

'The Mentiads are on our side!' marvelled Romana.

'I thought they would be,' the Doctor said, and she didn't know if he was making it up. 'We might be the best hope this planet has.'

'I don't understand,' said Kimus as the Mentiads led them away.

'Exciting, isn't it?' the Doctor grinned.

Behind them the curtain of energy remained shimmering as the Guards' guns bleated at it.

Mula and K-9 were inside the cavern.

K-9 looked up suddenly, excited. 'Master?'

'What is it?' asked Mula.

'The Mentiads have located the Doctor-Master,' K-9 informed her. 'They are approaching.'

'How can you tell? I can't hear anything.'

K-9 considered his answer. 'The Doctor has very distinctive heartbeats. Estimated time of arrival 21.9 seconds.'

Mula couldn't get over the Mentiads – her entire life she had been taught to hate and fear them, had been told that the Captain worked hard to keep them safe from the Mentiads. And she'd never known, never dreamed that the Mentiads were just people. The same as everyone else on Zanak. And now her brother had joined them.

K-9 had assured her that the Doctor would not have sent them here if it had been dangerous. Occasionally, K-9 permitted himself little white lies. The Doctor's approach to safety was questionable at best.

'But how could he know that they meant us no harm?'

'The Doctor-Master learned many things when they attacked him,' K-9 informed her. 'Subsequent analysis of their brainwave patterns indicated no malice when they attacked him.'

'You mean they slammed him to the wall with good vibrations?'

'Affirmative.' 19.3 seconds had passed. 'Arrival imminent.'

The Mentiads strode into their cavern. Mula tried her best not to flinch at them – their pallbearer demeanour, their pale faces, their dead eyes. They brought with them Kimus, Romana, and the Doctor.

'Hello, K-9, surprised to see us?'

'Amazed, Master.'

'There you are!' Delighted, the Doctor turned to the Mentiads, clearly in his element. 'Didn't I say he'd be amazed?'

A Guard ran onto the Bridge, breathless.

Mr Fibuli put down his clipboard. The Nurse paused in taking the Captain's temperature. Something in the Guard's demeanour did not suggest good news.

'Captain? Sir?'

The Captain remained staring out at the new sky. 'Speak! Are our visitors deceased?'

'We were attacked in the mines, sir.' The Guard's terror was plain.

'Attacked?' The Captain finally turned. He took one single, very loud step towards the Guard, pistons hissing.

'The Doctor – they escaped with the Mentiads.'

'With the Mentiads?' The Captain's voice sank to a menacing purr. Mr Fibuli and the Nurse exchanged glances. This was very bad news.

It took every last bit of courage for the Guard to not run away.

The Captain leaned in, confiding a little secret to him. 'Incompetent fool,' he muttered.

The Polyphase Avatron swooped down from his shoulder, extruded its laser and made short, horrible work of the Guard.

The Captain turned back to the sky, thoughtful. If the strangers knew the secret of Zanak, and had united with the Mentiads then his plans had suddenly become more complicated.

The Nurse appeared at his side, solicitous.

Behind them both, Mr Fibuli couldn't take his eyes off the Guard's boot, twitching as its owner finally died.

*

The Doctor was sitting cross-legged on the floor, the cloud of glowing dust dancing around him. The Mentiads had drawn around him.

Finally their leader – the oldest, palest, and saddest of the Mentiads – spoke. 'Doctor, do you bring us the understanding we seek? For generation upon generation our planet has been assailed by a nameless evil. We would know its name.'

The Doctor frowned. 'Its name is the Captain, you know that. Why haven't you kicked him out?'

The Mentiads shuffled, not meeting each other's eyes. 'The Captain's evil is beyond our comprehension,' their leader continued. 'Strange images haunt our brains. When a new Mentiad appears amongst the people, we know we must find them.'

'They found me in time,' said Pralix.

'With each new soul who joins us, we grow stronger, but still the understanding evades us.' The leader made a helpless shrug. 'The hatred of the people constrains us.'

The Doctor nodded, ideas assembling in his head. 'You're a telepathic gestalt,' he said.

'A what?' asked Kimus.

K-9, sensing a definition was required, glided forward. 'Many minds combined together telepathically to form a single entity.'

Romana nodded. It made sense to her. 'The power of a gestalt can be enormous.' They had something similar on Gallifrey – a vast space where the memories of dead Time Lords gathered to grumble.

Pralix took Mula's hand. His hand was so cold, but she did her best not to recoil.

'Can you help us, Doctor?' Pralix asked. 'We are powerless unless we understand. Can you tell us what's happening to Zanak?'

Oh dear, thought Romana. This is going to require tact and discretion.

'Yes. Zanak's just a shell, a completely hollow planet,' said the Doctor.

Romana bit her lip.

'Hollow?' Mula looked alarmed. The Mentiads didn't look pleased either.

'Hollow, but very rarely empty,' the Doctor continued. 'There are vast transmat engines hidden underneath the Captain's mountain.'

Romana took over, explaining carefully how the engines moved Zanak around in space. 'You don't notice it, of course, because you are part of the transmat field, so you stay with it. But in the same instant Zanak vanishes, it materialises in a different part of the galaxy around another, slightly smaller planet. Most recently Calufrax.'

The Doctor reasserted himself. He wasn't sure he cared for how well Romana was doing this. 'So your planet—'

'Zanak,' put in Romana, beaming. 'Just helping you along, Doctor.'

'Yes. So your planet—'

'Zanak,' Mula said the name again. The Doctor wanted to chide her, but her face was almost as ashen as her brother's.

The Doctor had the Mentiads' full attention as he explained a mystery that had been lurking at the corner of their minds for generations, and told them the awful origin of their powers. 'So, having materialised around the other planet, Zanak smothers it, crushes it and mines all the mineral wealth from it – extinguishing all life in the process.'

Kimus remembered what the Doctor had said. 'And that's when the lights change?'

'The stars, yes,' said the Doctor.

'The Omens!' Mula tried to remember how often the lights had changed in her lifetime. So many times.

'That's right.' The Doctor nodded. 'The Omens means the death of another planet.'

The Captain had been very cross all afternoon. All the Guards had been brought up from the mines, and their executions had only slightly cheered the Captain.

The Nurse fussed over him, checking the readings on her little black box while he ranted.

'Do you know what my problem is, Mr Fibuli?' The Captain glared out of the window until the twin suns backed away a little. 'By the blood of the Sky Demon, but we've been queasy fools! We should have obliterated the Mentiads years ago and rid ourselves of their sickly power.'

'But Captain,' Mr Fibuli pointed out reasonably, 'we have tried many times in the past …'

'And failed Mr Fibuli, and failed!'

The robot parrot fixed him with a warning glare.

Mr Fibuli's eyes wandered over to the pile of corpses and then switched back to the sky. 'Captain, you said yourself it was a question of priorities …'

'*I* said? You dare to lay the rotting fruits of your own incompetence at *my* door?' The Captain staggered to his feet, looming over his hapless aide. The robot parrot perked up decidedly.

The Nurse laid a gentle, restraining hand on the Captain's arm. It rested just out of reach of the bird's beak. The Captain looked at her, like a child pleading for another go on his favourite ride. The Nurse shook her head.

Quickly, Mr Fibuli pressed home his advantage. 'Captain, in your wisdom you observed that whilst the Mentiads lay dormant with no leader and no purpose we were well enough protected, and they were a useful focus for the fear of the people.'

'But now they will not be leaderless!' the Captain rumbled furiously. 'Now they will have a clear purpose.'

'But Captain.' Mr Fibuli had his moments of quicksilver cunning. 'The means to destroy them is at last within our grasp. The planet of Calufrax is rich in Voolium and Madranite 1–5. That is, after all, what we came here for.'

'Voolium and Madranite 1–5?' The Captain awkwardly stroked his chin. 'That is true.'

'The vibrations of the refined crystals can be harnessed to produce interference patterns which will neutralise the power of the Mentiads.'

The Captain gurgled with delight. 'That will leave them defenceless, as weak as ordinary men, obliterable! Oh, excellent, Mr Fibuli, excellent!'

The Nurse risked an encouraging smile in Mr Fibuli's direction.

The Captain continued: 'Your death shall be delayed.'

'Thank you again and again, sir.' Mr Fibuli hoped he didn't sound too dry. 'Your goodness confounds me.'

'How soon can you be prepared?' The Captain was shifting from one foot to another with an eager clank.

Mr Fibuli was already scribbling away on his pad. 'Well, if we put all the automated mining and processing equipment on the planet into full power, sir, we could reduce the entirety of Calufrax within hours, but the machinery will be dangerously overloaded …' He tore out a scrap of paper and handed it to the Captain.

'That matters not a quark, Mr Fibuli!' The Captain screwed the paper into a ball. 'Speed is of the essence! The Mentiads will be moving even now! Do it on the instant! This time there shall be no escape for them – nor for the Doctor!'

*

The Doctor had demanded everyone tell him the history of Zanak. That would have worked better, thought Romana, if he didn't keep interrupting. Still, she found it a fascinating example of socio-archetypal development in a post-agrarian demagogic state.

Kimus kept trying to make speeches against the social order, while Mula made small, practical observations. The Mentiads offered little – an almost perfect objective correlative to their being full of power but unable to express it. Pralix was doing his best to speak for them, but you could already see him becoming swamped in their shared mental burden.

'So Zanak was a happy, prosperous planet?' the Doctor asked.

'Yes, till the reign of Queen Xanxia,' said Pralix.

'May her spirit be accursed!' That, naturally, was Kimus.

'She had some kind of evil powers.' Mula smiled bashfully, recounting a folk story. 'Legends say she lived for hundreds of years.'

'That's not necessarily evil. I've known hundreds of people who've lived for hundreds of years,' the Doctor muttered.

Romana nudged him in the elbow. 'Do go on,' she encouraged the group.

At which point K-9 bleeped with a warning.

The Doctor theatrically shushed him. 'Ignore my dog. Always interrupting. Very annoying. Please carry on.'

'Queen Xanxia staged galactic wars to demonstrate her powers,' Mula continued.

'By the time she'd finished, Zanak was ruined!' Kimus proclaimed.

'When the Captain arrived, there was hardly anyone left alive,' Pralix said.

'Just a few miserable nomadic tribes,' the ancient leader of the Mentiads spoke, his voice broken by time.

'And how did the Captain arrive?' the Doctor wondered.

'Legend speaks of a giant silver ship that fell from the sky one night with a mighty crash like thunder,' Pralix said.

The Mentiads nodded. 'The Captain was one of the few survivors,' the oldest Mentiad groaned.

'And needed pretty extensive surgery, by the look of him,' the Doctor mused. 'I wonder who did that?'

Even Kimus shrugged.

'I don't think anyone knows,' Pralix apologised.

'Master?' K-9 tried again.

'Not now, K9, not now,' the Doctor snapped. 'Do go on.'

'The Captain took charge of Zanak,' the oldest Mentiad continued, his voice so weak everyone leaned forward to catch at it. 'He persuaded the people to work for him.'

'Golden ages of prosperity!' Kimus sneered. 'Pampered slavery, more like.'

99

'And then,' the oldest Mentiad gave a sigh of falling leaves, 'for some of us, terrible agonies of the mind began.'

'They would for someone who had latent telepathic ability, wouldn't they, Romana?'

Romana seized at the opportunity. 'You were absorbing what you would call the life force from the plundered planets.'

The Doctor gave her a little nod.

'What is the life force?' Pralix asked.

'Well, er, well ...' The Doctor dried. 'It's quite difficult to explain in simple terms, but, um, you'll tell them, won't you, Romana?'

Resisting the urge to roll her eyes, she smiled pleasantly. 'Every atom of matter in the universe has a certain amount of energy locked inside it. With something the size of a planet, there's an enormous quantity ...'

'Absolutely enormous!' the Doctor chimed in. Of course he did.

'So every time Zanak crushes a planet,' Romana went on, 'it releases that energy. Some of it will be on psychic wavelengths. Every time that happens, there's a fantastic blast of psychic energy, enough to smash open the neural pathways of anyone with telepathic abilities. Like you Mentiads.'

'You Mentiads were absorbing all that power into your brains,' the Doctor said, aghast.

'And each planet as it dies, adds to that power?' the oldest Mentiad groaned.

The other Mentiads shifted on the ground. They now knew the origin of the power that crushed them, swamped their minds.

'The death agonies of worlds!' Kimus shouted, unhelpfully. 'And the power by which they will be avenged.'

'Master?' K-9 interjected a third time.

'Oh, what is it?' the Doctor groaned, although in truth he was quite grateful for his dog ruining Kimus's moment.

K-9 cleared its throat. 'My seismograph detects enormous increase in mining operations round the whole planet. Every mining machine is now working at full pressure.'

Zanak shook. On the planet's surface, the waters rippled and the sands stirred. The shaking increased as you went up the mountain until you reached the Citadel. The entire Bridge was in turmoil as the engines threw their full force into devouring the planet Calufrax. A noise filled the Bridge. The sound of a world screaming.

At first, Mr Fibuli thought that the Captain was whistling while he worked. Then he realised it was the Polyphase Avatron, chirruping as it hopped across the table, eagerly pecking its way through the circuit boards piling up around the Captain. Both man and pet were content; the Captain was working on a circuit board, retracing the connections between impossibly precious stones. He was in a reflective mood that seemed almost happy.

'Why, by the left frontal lobe of the Sky Demon, Mr Fibuli, I was one of the greatest hyper-engineers of my time.'

'Indeed, Captain, your reconstruction of this planet is proof of that.' Mr Fibuli's flattery was sincere.

The Captain tapped the component. 'It is not scale that counts, Mr Fibuli, but skill. Now, the ship from which most of the major components were salvaged, the *Vantarialis* ... Now there was a ship ...' He pushed away his work and stood up. Motioning Mr Fibuli to follow him, he crossed to the dome, gazing out at the world beyond the mountain. If he was looking at anything, it was somewhere a long way beyond the view. 'The *Vantarialis* was the greatest raiding cruiser ever built, and I made it with technology so advanced you would not be able to distinguish it from magic.'

Mr Fibuli humbly agreed with a bow. 'All the same, sir, Zanak must be one of the great engineering feats of all time. A hollow, space-jumping planet?'

'This planet? This vile, lumbering planet?' The ruminative Captain was swept away by the familiar rage. 'Devil storms, Mister Fibuli, you are a callow fool! Do you not see how my heart burns for the dangerous liberty of the skies? Plunder, battle, and escape! My soul is imprisoned, bound to this ugly lump of blighted rock, beset by zombie Mentiads and interfering Doctors.'

'But what can they do to you, Captain?'

'Enough!' The Captain's fist thudded into the edge of the dome. 'They shall die! By the flaming moons of Hell, they shall die.' He marched back to his workbench and resumed work. 'Bring me the crystals, Mr Fibuli!'

Mr Fibuli bowed and scurried away.

'I shall be avenged!' the Captain muttered to himself.

A softly restraining hand landed on his shoulder. It was the Nurse. She glanced politely at his project. 'How lovely! I see you've found some occupational therapy. It's a good thing not to let your old skills die.'

The ghost of a smile twitched at the Captain's tin lips. 'Oh, I assure you, my old skills are very much alive ...'

'Well,' said the Doctor, ready to show off, 'they say you can fool some of the people all of the time. Let's see, shall we?'

Crouched by a pillar in the square, he neatly bowled a bag of liquorice allsorts. They arced across the square and scattered across the bonnet of an air-car, causing the Guard inside to leap out. Glaring around at the square, he drew his gun and headed off into the shadows.

The Guard didn't realise that the Doctor had already slipped into the air-car, dragging an excited Kimus with him.

103

'I really must stop doing this,' the Doctor sighed. 'It's like taking fish from a baby.'

At which point he touched the controls, and found himself glued to them by an agonising electrical field.

The Guard took his time to come back to them, his gun raised.

'Hands up, Kimus,' the Doctor said through clenched teeth. He tried to lift his own from the controls without success. He flashed the Guard a winning grin. 'I'm terribly sorry. Could you help me surrender?'

Chapter Eight

The Trophy Room

Mr Fibuli was cautiously deciding that today was going to be a good day after all. 'Captain, sir! Captain, they've caught the Doctor!

'Splendid, Mr Fibuli!' The Captain slotted another jewel into place.

'He was trying to steal an air-car, but one of our Guards immobilised it. We've sent another air-car to pick them up …'

'Ha!' The Captain bellowed, his breath reeking of chops fried in diesel. 'Trivia, Mr Fibuli, pleasant trivia. Have the Guards managed to open his vessel yet?'

Well now, there was still some bad news left in the world, reflected Mr Fibuli. 'His craft is proving remarkably difficult. Nothing they can do will even mark it.'

'Fools. Incompetents.'

Mr Fibuli held up some star charts. 'But we have located a potential source for PJX18.'

'Ah. Better, Mr Fibuli.' The Captain grinned.

Mr Fibuli offered a clipboard. 'I've calculated we can manage one more jump under our present conditions, sir. If we made it to that planet, we could mine it for PJX18 and then make our own repairs.'

'Then we will mine it!' The Captain addressed the crew: 'Prepare to jump as soon as the Voolium and Madranite 1–5 crystals have been produced. You know, it's all coming together marvellously, Mr Fibuli.'

Mr Fibuli had a small note to make. 'I feel I should point out, sir, that it is a heavily populated planet ...'

'Show me the chart!' The Captain unrolled it across a workbench.

Mr Fibuli wafted a hesitant finger at a small blue-green dot on the chart. 'It is here, sir, in the planetary system of the star Sol. The planet Terra.'

'A pretty planet.' Was there a trace of regret in the Captain's voice? Did the robot parrot repeat the phrase softly?

Mr Fibuli handed over a mineral report. Perhaps his master was wavering? 'It does indeed appear to be a pleasant world, Captain.'

'Then it will be pleasant to destroy it.' The Captain let go of the chart, and it rolled up with a snap.

'Yes, sir,' Mr Fibuli sighed. 'I shall make arrangements.'

The Nurse appeared with some medication. 'Another planet, Captain?'

'Yes,' the Captain grated. 'Another planet.'

'Then your objective will soon be reached, won't it?' she said soothingly as she started to check the Captain's vital signs against the readings on her black box.

The Captain snorted with laughter. 'It will. It will indeed.'

Romana had put K-9 to work. The Doctor and Kimus had gone off to confront the Captain. Romana had gone with Mula to back them up, leaving K-9 trying to interface with the systems of Zanak. The robot dog was currently plugged into a streetlamp.

The dog paused in his work. Information was pulsing through the computers of Zanak. Disagreeable but highly predictable information.

'Master?'

The dog unplugged himself from the lamp and set off to find an air-car. The Doctor-Master was in trouble.

Romana and Mula and Pralix were at the front of a procession of Mentiads. They were heading up the mountain to find a way into the Citadel.

Mula kept sneaking worried glances at her brother. He seemed at peace but somehow empty. His eyes were sunken into his face, his teeth clamped firmly shut. As though he were in terrible pain and trying not to cry out.

Romana gave her an encouraging look. Although she'd not been travelling with the Doctor for long she knew that he could change the fate of an entire planet within hours. Whatever else you could say about the Doctor, you had to admit he was a force to be reckoned with.

A force to be reckoned with was currently out cold and dreaming, busily settling a few old scores. 'And how many times do I have to tell you, no Janis thorns?'

The Doctor woke up. In his first blink he realised he was chained up on the Bridge. In his second blink he diagnosed that he'd been knocked unconscious. With his third blink he found Kimus crumpled beside him, and by the fourth blink he figured he should acknowledge the Captain looming over him.

'Good morning!' the Doctor beamed. Unable to wave, he jiggled his manacles.

The Captain was, the Doctor realised, gloating. He couldn't abide a gloater, especially not one with a killer robot parrot on his shoulder.

'So, Doctor, you have discovered the little secret of our planet.'

'You won't get away with it, you know.' The Doctor's smile faded and for a moment he was deadly serious.

'And what makes you so certain of that?'

'At the moment? Nothing at all, but it does my morale no end of good just to say it. I've been tied to pillars by better men than you, Captain.'

The Captain grinned like a broken bin. 'Ah, but none, I dare guess, more vicious.' A single metal hand twisted the Doctor's manacles, the metal clumping together into a ball.

The Doctor gasped. 'Vicious? You? Ha!' he sneered.

The Captain leaned in closer, steam leaking from his joints. 'I can be very vicious indeed, Doctor.'

The Doctor turned to a still unconscious Kimus. 'Don't panic, Kimus. Don't panic.'

He may have been chained up with a literally tin-pot dictator, but he was learning things, and the Doctor did so enjoy having an enquiring mind.

'What are you doing it for, Captain?' He was using his best Be Reasonable tone. 'It doesn't make sense and you know it. I can understand the life of a full-blooded pirate, the thrill, the danger, the derring-do, but this? Hiding away in your mountain retreat whilst you hop through space eating other people's perfectly good planets? Where's the derring-do in that?'

'Silence!'

The Doctor grinned. 'You're just trying to shut me up. You can't kill me whilst I'm tied up, can you?'

'Oh, can't I?' the Captain leered.

'No, you can't.' The Doctor could gloat as much as the Captain. 'You're a warrior and it's against a warrior's code.' He winked. 'You should have thought of that before you got out the manacles.'

'By the Hounds of Hell!' The Captain drew back his arm, hand bunched into a metal fist.

The Doctor managed not to flinch. 'Hard to listen, isn't it, Captain, when someone's touching a nerve? But what are you after here? I assume you don't want to take over the universe, do you? No, you wouldn't know what to do with it, beyond shouting at it.'

There was a ghastly silence on the Bridge.

The Captain glared at the Doctor, steam leaking between his metal teeth.

'Well?' demanded the Doctor, glaring back.

The Captain gave a sudden snort. Was it a laugh or fury? 'Mr Fibuli!'

'Yes, sir?' the worried man came scuttling up.

The Captain jerked a thumb towards the Doctor. 'Release him.' Then he strode from the Bridge.

Mr Fibuli stared at the Doctor in alarm.

The Doctor grinned back at him.

'But, Captain ...' began Mr Fibuli.

'You heard what he said.' The Doctor's tone was casual. 'He said release me.'

The Captain was waiting for the Doctor in his Trophy Room – a gallery that ran around the edges of the dome. Inset into the glass walls of the dome were little cases. They were, at first glance, slightly twee. The sort of cabinets where you might keep swimming trophies, or little plates with painted kittens.

The Doctor leaned close. No. No painted kittens.

Each cabinet contained a small model of a planet, hovering in mid air, glowing gently. These were all the worlds consumed by Zanak. At one level the artistry

110

was exquisite; at another it was ghastly. It was like standing in a graveyard orrery.

The Doctor was standing in front of a model of Bandraginus Five. So realistic it looked as though you could simply fly down onto it. Someone had taken the care to very neatly label the exhibits. In his experience, very neat labelling was the sure sign of a maniac.

'My trophies, Doctor. Feast your eyes on them, for they represent an achievement unparalleled in the universe.'

'Tombstones? Memorials to all the worlds you've destroyed?' The Doctor wasn't going to let the Captain have this victory.

'Not memorials. These are the entire remains of the worlds themselves.'

'What?' The Doctor stared at the spheres spinning in their cabinets.

'I come in here to dream of freedom.'

The Doctor should have been listening to this, but the enormity of what he'd been told had exploded in his head, and he could only hear the ringing in his ears. 'Excuse me, did you say these are the entire remains of the worlds themselves?'

'Yes, Doctor!' The Captain tapped the cabinet labelled Viskon Alpha. 'Each of these small spheres is the crushed remains of a world. Millions upon millions of tons of compressed rock held suspended here by forces beyond the limits of the imagination, forces that I have generated and harnessed.'

'But that's impossible!' Staring at the trophies around him, the Doctor experienced a terrible urge to run away screaming. 'That amount of matter in that small a space would undergo instant gravitational collapse and form a black hole.'

'Precisely, Doctor.' The Captain was enjoying himself.

'But Zanak would be dragged into a gravitational whirlpool.'

'And why isn't it?' The Captain had climbed to a whole new level of smugness. 'Because the whole system is so perfectly aligned by the most exquisite exercise in gravitational geometry that every force is balanced out within the system! Which is why we can stand next to billions of tons of super-compressed matter and not even be aware of it.' He stroked the surface of a cabinet. 'With each new planet I acquire—'

'*Acquire?*' The Doctor's jaw fell open.

'– the forces of my exhibit are meticulously realigned, but the system remains stable.'

'If what you say is true—'

'Oh, it is.'

'Then,' whispered the Doctor, 'it is the most brilliant piece of astro-gravitational engineering I have ever seen … It's a staggering concept. Pointless, but staggering.'

'I am gratified that you appreciate it,' purred the Captain.

'Appreciate it? *Appreciate it?*' The Doctor got this far and then, just for once, was lost for words. He jabbed a finger at poor Bandraginus Five. 'You commit mass destruction and murder on a scale that is almost inconceivable and you ask me to appreciate it? Just because you happen to have made a brilliantly conceived mathematical toy out of the mummified corpses of planets—!'

'Devil storms, Doctor!' The Captain advanced on him, annoyed rather than angry. 'This is not a toy!'

'Then what is it for?' The Doctor was nearly screaming. 'What are you doing? What can possibly be worth all this?'

The Captain flung the Doctor up against a cabinet. It was empty, all neatly labelled and waiting to hold its memento mori. It was labelled 'Calufrax'. The Doctor found his head rammed into a space meant to contain an entire world, the force field buzzing agonisingly around his ears.

The Captain leaned very close, his voice soft. 'By the raging fury of the Sky Demon, Doctor, you ask too many questions. You have seen! You have admired! But you have not thought. Be satisfied and ask no more.'

Furious, the Captain yanked the Doctor's head out of the cabinet. The Doctor fell gasping to the floor.

'No one understands me ...' Muttering in disgust to himself, the Captain turned away.

Mr Fibuli's voice came over a loudspeaker, telling him he was needed on the Bridge as the Mentiads were coming.

The Doctor tried not to beam delightedly.

Surprisingly, the Captain threw back his head and laughed. 'Excellent, Mr Fibuli, that is simply excellent.' He gestured for some Guards to collect the Doctor.

This was not quite what the Doctor had expected. Lying on the floor, he knew he had disappointed the Captain somehow. He looked up at the tortured remains of planets ranged along the wall. There was something about them, something he could almost name, almost measure. And yet …

'What am I missing?' he wondered.

By Romana's rough calculations they were 47.3 per cent up the mountain, and the slopes were looking steeper. 'It's a long climb up there.'

'Don't worry, we'll make it,' Pralix said. The Mentiads nodded encouragingly. Romana felt a flicker of worry – what if she was just leading these people into a massacre?

'I hope Kimus and the Doctor managed to break into the Engine Room without getting caught,' said Mula. She hoped Kimus hadn't let the Doctor down.

'We're in trouble if they haven't,' agreed Pralix.

'Don't worry,' said Romana with a weak-orange-squash smile. 'The Doctor knows what he's doing.'

Chapter Nine

Life's Fleeting, but Plank's Constant

The Doctor was carried onto the Bridge. He looked up at his guards. 'Would you care to put me down over there?'

They dropped him onto the floor. All around him was an air of bustle. He liked an air of bustle. Especially from the opposition. It usually told him they were about to lose.

The Captain sat at a desk, tinkering with a piece of equipment. He whistled while he worked, his parrot joining in. 'Doctor! We're preparing to meet your friends, the Mentiads. The poor misbegotten fools who are going to attempt to storm the Bridge.'

'That should be fun.' The Doctor had high hopes for the Mentiads. Of course, in order for them to succeed, he and Kimus would need to have disabled the engines. Hadn't quite got there yet, but it had been a crowded day. Still time, still time.

Kimus woke up at last, looked around, and muttered a single word: 'What?'

Fair enough, thought the Doctor. 'Kimus, are you all right?'

Kimus groaned weakly. The Captain's Guards had enjoyed silencing his revolutionary opinions.

The Doctor gestured to the rebel. 'For goodness sake, get him down. He hasn't done you any harm.'

'Oh, you do it,' said the Captain with surprisingly casualness. He threw a key on the floor.

The Doctor reached out for it, and the Captain's foot landed with the expert force of a steam press on his hand.

The Captain and the Time Lord regarded each other. The Doctor hissed with pain. The Captain twisted his lips in a tin smirk and, with an agonising twist of his boot, strode away.

The Doctor cradled his fingers, blowing on them. Then he set about freeing Kimus.

The young rebel was trying his best to take his surroundings in, but they were almost entirely alien to him. 'Doctor, where, where are we?'

'On the Bridge.'

'And what's that?' Kimus was staring in puzzled horror at the figure of the Captain.

'That's your beloved Captain.'

Kimus couldn't quite believe his eyes. It was one thing to say the Captain was a monster. It was another thing to discover that he actually was. He couldn't take his eyes off the figure, the tiny bits of man jammed haphazardly between slices of tin, wrapped in the odour of a butcher's bin on a sunny day.

'But—' began Kimus, and he put a lot of feeling into that *But*.

'Don't make any noise,' the Doctor whispered. 'The Mentiads are on their way here and the Captain's got no power against their psychic strength.'

'What's that machine he's working on?' Kimus was trying to process everything.

'Oh, it looks like a Psychic Interferometer.'

'What's one of those?'

'Well, it's a sort of machine for blocking psychic power ...'

The Doctor and Kimus stared at each other in horror.

There was a chuckle.

The Captain was watching them.

'Indeed,' he agreed, holding his device up. 'Wag your tongue well, Doctor. Once I neutralise your army of telepaths, your tongue will be the only weapon you have left.'

The Doctor had spotted a flaw in this plan. 'Well, that's nonsense. To make that machine work you'd need a collection of extremely rare crystals.' He adopted a lecturing tone. 'Such as Voolium and Madranite 1–5. And they only occur on one planet I know of, and that's ... er ... It'll come back to me ...'

Mr Fibuli rushed onto the Bridge, carrying a small wooden box. 'Captain, here are the crystals from—'

'Calufrax,' the Doctor sighed miserably. 'Oh dear. My biorhythms must be at an all-time low.'

The Captain laughed an almost good-natured laugh. He plucked the crystals from the box and plugged them into his device. Each crystal began to glow and the robot parrot clucked happily as the power grew within the Interferometer.

'Doctor, your friends are doomed!' announced the Captain.

'Are they?'

'And so are you,' the Captain announced after a moment's deliberation. 'We need not delay your death any longer. By the curled fangs of the Sky Demon, I have looked forward to this moment.' He whistled at his robot parrot, and it flew up from his shoulder, eyes glowing dangerously.

Imminent death gave Kimus a spurt of courage. He rushed forward, grabbing up a chair as a weapon. 'You hideous, deformed, murdering maniac!'

He swung it against the Captain's body. There was a dull, empty clang. He swung it again, connecting with the shoulder. There was another thud.

Kimus beat the chair against the Captain again and again. The problem was there was so much of him to hit. And yet also so very little.

'Kimus …' the Doctor said gently.

'Finished?' the Captain asked, surprisingly mildly.

Kimus looked up at the Captain, his cheeks burning with shame. He had tried, and he had failed.

'Avatron.' The Captain turned to his parrot. 'Kill them both.'

The Avatron swooped down on the Doctor and Kimus. Its eyes were glowing, its talons buzzing with electricity.

As the Doctor and Kimus threw themselves across the Bridge, no one noticed the great door opening. This was far too much fun. The Captain's crew watched, jeering and placing bets as the bird feinted, swooped and pounced. It was toying with its prey.

'I'm going to be killed by a robot parrot,' the Doctor muttered, hurling himself through the air. 'What a way to go.'

Kimus cried out as a talon raked him, and a blast sizzled the edge of the Doctor's hair. He landed awkwardly in a heap, and something shoved him out of the way of another blast. Shoved him out of the way and shot forward, firing at the parrot.

It was K-9.

The Doctor considered his luck, for the very briefest of moments. Then grabbed hold of Kimus and bolted for the door.

The Polyphase Avatron paused mid-swoop. For a moment the robot dog and the robot parrot glared at each other. They sized each other up and picked a size that wasn't flattering.

Having finally located the nagging interference with his systems, K-9 emitted a noise that sounded, just a little, like a growl.

The crew ducked for cover as the air exploded with fire. Only the Captain stood his ground, watching the combat around him and laughing.

There were scratch marks down K-9's flank.

A metal feather fell to the floor.

The Captain's pet went soaring after the Doctor and Kimus, into the depths of the Citadel. And K-9 zipped after it, firing as he went.

The Doctor and Kimus ran.

Now that the joy of being rescued from certain death had passed, the Doctor was doing some rapid reflection on the state of play. They were still being chased by a robot parrot … The Mentiads were coming, unaware that the Captain had built a jammer for their powers … And the Doctor had promised to take control of the engines. Things weren't good, but something would turn up.

They found themselves in the Captain's Trophy Room, the parrot swooping after them.

Kimus stared around and started to ask unhelpful questions. The Doctor dragged him on. He also tried to ignore the crossfire from K-9 and the parrot smacking into the collapsed planets, threatening to turn Zanak into a black hole. But he did less well at this.

'We need to find a way out of here,' he said, dragging Kimus past the Captain's trophies. There had to be a way out. They reached a door. A very locked door.

The Doctor went to work on it with his sonic screwdriver.

The Avatron and K-9 dived and darted at each other, the air hot with blasts and sparks.

The parrot was getting closer.

'We're trapped!' wailed Kimus.

'Never,' the Doctor lied.

The door sprang open and the Doctor pushed him through.

The chamber they stumbled into was very dark. At the centre of it was a raised dais. No good, in the Doctor's experience, had ever come of a raised dais. People would leave thrones on them, for a start. As they had in this case.

Sat on the throne was a woman so old she was little more than a skeleton covered in tissue-paper skin. Face crumpled like rotten fruit, hair falling in rat tails over features which time had reduced to gnarled lumps. The face had once – perhaps – been beautiful, but all that remained was cruelty.

'Who is that?' Kimus reached out to touch the figure, but the Doctor stayed his hand.

'No. She's behind Time Dams.' The Doctor pointed out two metal pillars placed on either side of the frozen figure. 'They stop time. Not completely, but they can slow down the flow of time in the space between them – given enough energy.' And they were famously hungry inventions. It was why they'd never really caught on. They were also very dangerous. Had Kimus's hand crossed the barrier, that would have been it for him.

Kimus was still pointing at the decrepit figure on the throne. 'But who is it?'

The Doctor's brain made a leap and landed on solid ground. 'That's your beloved queen, Xanxia.'

'Queen Xanxia's dead. She died after the Captain arrived.'

'Really?' The Doctor gestured at the tattered fabrics draped over the body. 'She's not dead. Just as close as you can get to dead while still being alive. The Time Dams have suspended her in the last few seconds of life.'

'Does she know we're here?'

The Doctor considered. 'No.' Just to make sure he clicked his fingers. No reaction.

He started to examine the Time Dams. Steady, patient pulses of energy flowed through them like the ticking of a clock. A worried expression crept onto his face and made itself at home.

On the Bridge, chaos reigned. Loud chaos, because at its heart was the Captain.

At some point the main door to the Bridge had been sealed. Possibly by the Doctor, more likely by the crossfire between the two fighting robot animals.

But the door was shut, and the Captain was throwing his Guards at the door. Literally throwing them.

'Open it!' he was roaring.

Mr Fibuli lurked well back, and found himself standing next to the Nurse. They usually avoided talking to each other. There was something about the Nurse which did not invite confidence. But just this once, Mr Fibuli found himself wanting to ask her if she was all right. She seemed nervous.

'It looks very shut,' he said. Bit of an icebreaker.

If she heard him, she did not acknowledge.

'How much longer must we wait?' she muttered.

'The situation is very bad indeed.' The Doctor took a step back from the frozen queen, shaking his head gravely. 'To find enough energy to fuel those dams, you'd need to ransack entire planets.'

'So whole other worlds have been destroyed with the sole purpose of keeping *that* alive?' Kimus stared at the creature on her throne. That was the truth behind his planet's deadly purpose. He'd only just learned that there were other worlds. Now he was discovering that countless worlds, billions of people, had all died, just to keep this one, tiny, frail old woman a moment or two away from death. 'Pointless,' he breathed.

'There must be something more to it than that,' the Doctor advised him.

'Really?'

'Would you go to those lengths just to stay alive?'

Kimus squinted again at the immobile queen. Were her eyes following him around the room, or was that just a trick of the light? 'To stay forever in that revolting condition? No.'

'No, not in that condition ... So in *what* condition?'

The Doctor's train of thought was interrupted.

Something was coming. The Doctor held up his hand.

The door to the chamber slid open again. There was an ominous whirr.

K-9 bumped in unsteadily but triumphantly, a very dead Polyphase Avatron clamped to his muzzle.

He ceremoniously dropped it at the Doctor's feet.

The Doctor tried to pick the bird up, but it was still hot. 'Well done, K-9, well done. Look at that, isn't that marvellous!'

'Your congratulations are ... un ... unnecessary, Master,' K-9 stuttered proudly.

The dog wasn't in very good shape, so the Doctor tried to cheer him up. 'You're a good dog. The best. A hero!'

The robot dog wagged a feeble tail.

'Well that's a relief,' said Kimus. 'But what do we do about the others? The Guards? How do we get out of here? And what are we doing about the Mentiads?'

'That's where the two of you can help.' The Doctor ruffled K-9's battered ears. 'Have you enough energy in you for one more mission?'

The dog paused, just slightly. 'Affirmative, Master.'

'Splendid.' The Doctor nodded to a steel door in the wall. 'Over there, there's a service lift. It must go down to the Engine Room.'

'Master?'

'Why don't you take Kimus with you down in the lift, find that Engine Room and sabotage the engines?'

A little drunkenly, the robot dog weaved towards the elevator.

'But what about you?' demanded Kimus.

'Ah …' The Doctor drew himself up, ready for action. He rifled through the toolkit by the Time Dams, glanced at a manual, tossed it to one side, then pocketed an interesting piece of machinery. 'I'm going to see the Captain.'

Two Guards had only just cleared the last of the debris away from the entrance when someone tapped them very politely on the shoulder.

'Gentlemen, good afternoon!' The Doctor beamed and cleared his throat. 'All right, all right, all right, I give up.'

The Guards brought the Doctor before the Captain who was sat in his command chair, flanked by the Nurse and Mr Fibuli.

The Captain was stroking the prongs of his beard. 'So, Doctor, you have survived.'

'I seem unable to break the habit.'

'And your friends?'

The Doctor's grin died, and he turned a thumb slowly down.

'Excellent. Killed by my Polyphase Avatron, no doubt.'

'Well, now.' The Doctor coughed, awkwardly pulling something out of his pocket and dropping it with a clang to the floor. It was the twisted remains of the Polyphase Avatron.

The Captain stared at it in horror and something inside him seemed to break.

'Destroyed?' He gave a barely stifled wail. He scooped the bird up, cradling the twisted wings. 'By the great parrot of Hades, Doctor, you shall pay with the last drop of your blood. Every corpuscle, do you hear?'

'I really am sorry about your pet,' the Doctor began. 'However—'

The Captain ignored him. 'Mr Fibuli!'

'Yes, sir?' Mr Fibuli bent over the Captain. So did the Nurse. They conferred.

The Doctor did not like the look of this. 'Captain? You'd better hear what I have to say. It's quite important.'

Mr Fibuli straightened up, and shook his head sadly. 'Guilty.'

'Guilty,' agreed the Nurse.

The Captain stood, bowed to them both, then turned to the Doctor. 'Guilty.'

'Listen to me,' the Doctor said. 'You're making a terrible mistake.'

The Captain pulled a lever on his desk and, at the centre of the Bridge, a pit sprang open. Projecting from the ledge was a plank. He shoved the Doctor towards it. 'Behold your death, Doctor!'

Well, thought the Doctor, at least this was novel.

'A plank,' said the Captain. 'The theory is very simple. You walk along it. At the end, you fall off and drop one thousand feet. Dead.'

'Really? You can't be serious.'

The Captain roared with laughter, slapping the Doctor on the back, with every indication that they were best friends. The slap pushed the Doctor towards the pit.

'Is he serious?' the Doctor asked of Mr Fibuli and the Nurse. They avoided his gaze.

The Doctor took a ginger step onto the plank. It wobbled beneath him. 'Captain, you don't realise what you're doing. Listen to me!'

'I shall listen to you when I hear you scream,' the Captain beamed at him.

The Doctor took another step. The pit beneath him was endlessly dark and the plank was now sagging with every edging movement he made. 'Please ... !' He held up a hand.

But the Captain drew a pistol, and a bolt of energy spat at the Doctor's feet. He jumped aside, lost his balance, missed his footing, and, in a tangle of limbs tumbled howling into the empty heart of Zanak.

'Bye-bye!' laughed the Captain.

Chapter Ten

Immortal Queen

The Captain and the Nurse stood watching the Doctor fall into the planet until they could see him no more. It was done.

Then the Captain started to laugh. The laugh spread to the Nurse, dutifully to Mr Fibuli, and then out across the Bridge.

Someone else joined in, laughing louder even than the Captain.

People looked around to see which doomed soul it was.

'Hello, everybody!' Lounging against a desk was the Doctor. He was juggling the crystals from the Captain's Psychic Interferometer.

For a moment, nobody said anything. Mr Fibuli marvelled that there was somehow enough of the Captain's face left to gawp.

'But—' the pirate managed eventually.

'Sorry I couldn't make the jump myself.' The crystals vanished into the Doctor's pockets and out came a small box. 'But I've got the most terrible head for heights.'

'Who? How?'

The Doctor flicked a switch on the device.

Another Doctor appeared, bouncing on the plank.

'Hello again!' he waved.

The Nurse thinned her lips.

'I've discovered your naughty little secret,' the copy addressed the room. 'We are not all quite as we seem to be, are we?'

'This is a remote holographic generator,' the other Doctor said. 'And the image it projects might almost be real.' He toggled the switch.

The holographic Doctor vanished from the plank, and reappeared in mid air, hovering over the abyss. 'Hello again again!'

'How are you doing, Doctor?' the real one asked.

'Can't complain. Bye-bye!' the hologram said, and vanished with a wave.

The Doctor turned to the room. 'Just as I was able to turn off that image of myself, I can turn off another apparently real person, can't I?'

Enjoying the tension creeping across the Bridge, the Doctor held up the device. Then he flicked a switch. 'I wonder which of us will disappear this time?'

All of a sudden, the Captain's Nurse flickered and vanished.

*

Romana had finally reached the doorway at the top of the mountain. She was explaining that this was the way into the Citadel. All they had to do was open the door.

Pralix lead the Mentiads in a burst of concentration. The door buckled, groaned, and then slid reluctantly open.

Romana and Mula exchanged impressed glances.

'My brother was never this useful before,' said Mula.

'You should see mine,' said Romana. She turned to the Mentiads. 'If we're going to rescue the Doctor, we'd better hurry.'

'The Doctor needs rescuing?' Mula frowned.

'Always, and mostly from himself.' Things were going rather well, Romana thought, preparing to leading the Mentiads into the mountain.

Which was when the Captain's Guards came for them – pouring out of the door and already firing. Several Mentiads fell screaming before Romana could shout a surrender. Feeling sick, she stared around wildly for cover.

It was no use. They were hopelessly outnumbered and outflanked, and it had all gone horribly wrong. They were going to die.

'Pralix!' cried Mula.

The Mentiads swept their gaze across the mountainside, causing it to slide away in a roaring tumble of boulders and Guards.

Romana stood, shaken and amazed, waiting for the dust and rubble to clear. There was no sign of the Guards. The rock fall had very neatly missed the entrance to the mountain.

'Very impressive,' Romana murmured.

The Mentiads shared a rather ghastly grin.

Mula pulled a weapon from a pile of rubble and strode towards the mountain. 'Coming?'

The figure of the Nurse flickered, and then reappeared. There was a new air of authority about her; the meekness had gone, replaced by a cruel smirk.

'You can try all you like, Doctor. It won't work.' The Nurse's simper was now a sneer. She stretched out her arms and examined them. 'My new body has almost attained fully corporeal form. I can no longer simply be turned off.' She snapped her fingers. 'Guards! Seize him!'

The Guards looked over at the Captain, who, remarkably, had slumped down into his chair and was trying to make himself look very small indeed. When he spoke it was with a sulky mumble. 'Do as she says.'

The Guards shrugged and seized the Doctor.

The Nurse walked over to him, surveying him with the leisurely predation of a well-fed cat towards a shrew. She reached into his pockets, took out the crystals, and passed them to Mr Fibuli.

Mr Fibuli, trying to work out what was going on, took them numbly. 'Who are you?' he asked her, before he could stop himself.

'What I have always been,' she told him. 'The power behind the throne.' She winked. 'Now, do put the Mandranite 1–5 in the Captain's device. He'll be ever so disappointed if he doesn't get to show it off.'

Mr Fibuli placed the crystals in the Psychic Interferometer and watched as they began to glow.

Romana saw the Guard before anyone else. He'd survived the rock fall, and scrambled over the edge of it, rifle raised. He opened fire, dropping three Mentiads before anyone could react.

Romana turned to the Mentiads, expecting to see the Guard knocked flat by a telepathic blast. Instead the Mentiads stood, mouths opening and closing like floundering fish.

'The power!' wailed Pralix. 'It's gone. Our power – we can't reach it.'

The Guard fired again, and two more Mentiads fell.

Mula raised her gun, aimed it, and then paused, uncertain of what to do with it.

Romana neatly took it from her, shot the Guard, then handed it back to her, looking around to assess the damage. 'Pralix – what happened?'

The Mentiads stared at each other in confusion. 'We can't tell. The contact between us has gone. We can no longer share or focus our energy.'

So much for the paranormal, thought Romana. Back to brute force.

Which was a problem. 'See if you can find any more guns,' she suggested, hopefully, nudging the fallen rocks with a delicate toe. This wasn't good – she was going up against a trained crew of pirates with a group of people who'd never fired a weapon in their lives. Ah well.

She led them into the mountain.

There was no ignoring the Nurse: the entire atmosphere of the Bridge had changed. She strode around it, utterly in command.

'Well?' she snapped. 'Is it working, Fibuli?'

'Yes,' he said hurriedly. 'The Interferometer is at full power.'

'Good!' The Nurse clapped her hands together. Her face lit up with a childish glee, and her voice gushed with enthusiasm. 'Now let's show these miserable zombies who really rules Zanak.'

'So ...' The Doctor cleared his throat, and winked at the Captain. 'Queen Xanxia, the tyrant Queen of Zanak. What about the real you – the wizened old body pinned between the Time Dams?'

'That thing is not me!' Xanxia spat furiously. '*This* is now me! Queen Xanxia reborn!'

She strode over to the Captain's chair. With a sullen scowl, the Captain got up and stood behind the chair. She sat in it.

'Only you're not the real Queen Xanxia quite yet, are you?' One of the Doctor's hobbies was failing to let tyrants down gently. 'I presume this new body of yours is based on a cell-projection system, isn't it?'

'It is.' The Nurse rallied. 'Permanent regeneration of cells synthesised from my old body, and thus containing all the memory patterns and all the brilliance built up over the centuries.'

'But it's still unstable, isn't it?' The Doctor tutted like she had served tepid soup. 'You're dependent on the last few seconds of life in the old body.'

The Nurse shrugged. 'I'm nearly complete. My molecular structure has almost bound together, finally and forever. That is why you could not turn me off.'

The Doctor held up a thumb and forefinger. 'You're this close. Sadly, that's as far as you're going to get. I'm an old hand at regenerations. It can't be done that way. Those Time Dams back there, they just won't work.'

The Nurse sneered at him. 'I have calculated every detail. I shall live for ever.'

'Bafflegab!' The Doctor rolled his eyes. 'I've never heard such bafflegab in all my lives.'

'You dare to mock me?'

'Easily.'

The Nurse proved her corporeality by slapping the Doctor hard in the face.

'Now we're getting somewhere.' The Doctor rubbed his jaw. Was the Captain really giving him a sympathetic look?

'And now you shall die for your insolence!' the Nurse announced.

The Doctor thought she was going to hit him again. Instead, her hand daintily stroked the little black box still slung around her shoulders.

For a moment nothing happened. Then the Captain lurched towards the Doctor, swiping the air menacingly. The lumbering steps continued, as inarticulate as a puppet. For the first time, the Doctor saw the man trapped inside the robotic body. The pirate had been mummified alive. The poor man had given up hope of rescue long ago.

'Captain! Listen to me,' the Doctor pleaded, backing away. 'This very much concerns you. How long has she been using you to do her dirty work? And what's your reward, Captain? Eternal life?'

Was he imagining it? Did that last step drag just a little?

'Eternal life?' sneered the Nurse. 'What do you know of eternal life?'

'Enough to know it can't be sustained by those Time Dams back there.'

'I'll prove you wrong,' sneered the Nurse as the Doctor leapt out of the Captain's way, keeping a desk between them. 'We'll see if you're still mocking when this body becomes fully corporeal.'

'Ah.' The Doctor slid under a desk as the Captain's fist smacked into it. 'But it never will become fully corporeal. Not ever.'

'I've done my calculations!'

'And got them wrong.' The Doctor was trying to seize the high ground while crawling along the floor.

'Impossible!' The Nurse stamped her foot, and gestured to the Captain to finish this now.

'Inevitable.' The Doctor flashed her the ghost of a grin. 'Because they're based on a false premise.'

'No! I've ransacked planets from Bandraginus to Calufrax! Do you think I'm going to stop now?'

The Doctor dodged another blow from the Captain and scrabbled towards the shelter of a computer. 'What's next? Will you steal suns? Will you try and convert entire galaxies into energy? Because you'll have to eventually, you know.' He dived out of the way as the Captain sent the computer crashing to the ground. 'There isn't enough energy in the universe to keep your Time Dams going for ever. In the end you *will* die.'

'You're lying!' the Nurse screamed. 'Lying to save your neck. Finish him, Captain!'

The Captain lurched towards the Doctor, fist raised and sparking with energy. The Doctor could see the Captain's jaw working, silently.

'You know what?' the Doctor told the Bridge. 'I don't think it's worth all this effort. What do you think, Mr Fibuli?' The meek man blushed. 'And you, Captain? What do you think?'

The Captain tried again to speak, and the Nurse stabbed at a button on her belt.

He froze, mid-swipe, robot arm hovering in the air. His one human eye was rolling furiously. The corner of his mouth was twitching. He seemed to be in terrible pain.

'Your little black box?' The Doctor tutted at the Nurse, suddenly feeling very sorry for the Captain. 'So that's how you control him.'

Alarms went off, ringing throughout the Bridge.

The Nurse took her hand off the black box and pointed to the door. 'That'll be the Mentiads. Captain! Deal with them!'

The Captain staggered, blinked, and took one halting step towards the door, before swinging round, lurching towards the Nurse, murder in his eye. He began to swear: 'By all the—'

Shrugging, the Nurse twisted the dial again, and the Captain froze, sparks surrounding him. The air filled with a greasy, warm smell.

'I said deal with them! Go on!' She released the button.

The Captain twisted away, letting out an agonised groan.

'Mr Fibuli,' the Captain croaked. 'Seal the Bridge.'

Mr Fibuli looked up at the tormented figure standing over him. 'Yes, Captain, of course, Captain,' he said gently, and pulled a lever. Steel bulkheads slammed down across all the entries to the Bridge.

Romana was feeling pretty pleased with her first insurgency. Admittedly, her troops were lacking weapons, but, if you looked at the big picture, she had managed to assemble a sizeable chunk of the local population and got them to climb a mountain, they had broken into the Captain's Citadel, and now they were all dead set on confronting him on the Bridge.

Well, up to a point. The Mentiads' sorrowful expressions had been replaced with a sort of weary agony as the life force built up inside them. A few of them held guns, but didn't seem to be paying much attention to the training Mula was giving them as Romana led them up into the Citadel. They passed down the ancient corridors until they reached the ruins of the Captain's ship, a jagged metal hatchway open at the far end of a courtyard dotted with dry fountains and statues of the same cruel woman made from precious stones. It was a sad, tasteless place – and, in tactical terms, looked to be dangerously open. Perhaps, if they kept to the cloisters and edged their way into the ship, they'd be fine.

Romana decided to give the Doctor the benefit of the doubt. He would, at any moment, disable the jammer and retake control of the Engine Room. And then they would win. It was how he worked. Seemingly shambolic, actually quietly in control all the time. She finally understood him, that impossible, wonderful man.

A spring in her step, Romana led the Mentiads through the courtyard, into the ship, and right up to the door to the Bridge. 'Now then!'

Romana banged on it. It was firmly sealed shut.

A squadron of Guards appeared at the far end of the courtyard behind them and opened fire.

'I get the feeling the Doctor's not in control here,' she sighed, ducking for cover.

The Doctor was reluctantly reaching the same conclusion.

'We are impregnable. The Mentiads are powerless, the Guards will pick them off at will. I control the engines, the Captain, and the entire planet,' announced the Nurse. The Doctor did so hate being kept alive purely to listen to a gloating summary. Or did the Nurse have another use for him?

She didn't even look round from her chair. She snapped her fingers. 'Captain, is Calufrax now entirely rendered?'

The Captain reached for a control, and then paused. 'Mr Fibuli?' he said, with a last trace of authority.

'Oh yes, sir,' his mate loyally hurried to confirm. 'All operations on Calufrax are now complete.'

The Nurse ignored the slight. 'Thank you, Mr Fibuli! And have you located a planet where we can find the mineral PJX18?'

'PJX18?' butted in the Doctor. 'That's quartz.'

'Yes,' clucked Mr Fibuli.

'But from where?'

Mr Fibuli consulted a star chart. 'It is found on the planet Terra in the star system Sol.'

'Captain, we will mine that planet immediately!' commanded the Queen. 'Prepare to jump.'

'Earth?' This really was too much for the Doctor. 'Do you really mean to go on with this madness? Captain, the Earth is an inhabited planet.'

Mr Fibuli sighed, then busied himself issuing orders. The Nurse spun round in the Captain's chair to gaze out through the dome at the sky beyond. Only the Captain met the Doctor's eye.

'Billions and billions of people. You can't be that insane.'

The Captain responded with a low groan.

The Nurse snapped her fingers again. 'Jump immediately, Captain. Jump!'

The Doctor looked at the Captain, pleading.

'It'll take ten minutes to set the coordinates,' the Captain's voice was flat.

'Eight minutes,' admitted Mr Fibuli, already inputting the coordinates.

The Captain groaned again.

The Doctor, hearts in his mouth, took a step back towards the door. And then another one.

The Captain said nothing.

'You can't possibly succeed. The Mentiads will destroy you.' The Doctor continued to edge towards the door, reaching out for the lever.

When the Captain failed to reply, Mr Fibuli spoke without looking up from his clipboard. 'Not while we have the Psychic Interferometer.'

'You mean this?' the Doctor pointed to it. It was just out of reach. Instead, he engaged the door control. It opened silently and the Doctor offered up a prayer to whoever oiled the hinges.

Mr Fibuli glanced over at the crystal lattice. 'Yes quite. Whilst the Interferometer is fully operational, the Mentiads are powerless. Wait, who opened the doors?'

'It's all right, I'll close them,' the Doctor offered.

'Thank you,' said Mr Fibuli, returning to his work.

'On my way out,' the Doctor added softly. With a small bow to the Captain, he slipped off the Bridge. As the door closed behind him, he heard the Nurse shout with anger. And grinned.

Romana was surprised to see the Doctor strolling out of the ship into the courtyard and straight into the middle of the gunfight.

'Hello everyone!' He ducked into the cloister and joined the Mentiads hiding behind a colonnade. Romana and Mula were keeping the Captain's Guards back as best as they could.

'Where are Kimus and K-9?' the Doctor asked as blasts chipped away at their shelter.

'Weren't they with you?'

'I sent them to sabotage the engines.' The Doctor looked around, just in case he'd miscounted. 'This planet's about to jump again.'

'And,' Romana said as the colonnade took another hit, 'we're fighting a losing battle here. The Mentiads can't seem to get their psychokinetic powers to work.'

'Ah.' The Doctor peered round the corner, and ducked back from a shot. 'I know. There's a Psychic Interferometer on the Bridge.'

Mula squeezed off a couple of blasts.

Kimus came running towards them across the courtyard, exhausted and covered in grime. He was waving frantically as he dodged the crossfire.

The Doctor beamed. Here was good news at last. The engines!

'It's no use, Doctor,' Kimus gasped, staggering into his arms. 'The Engine Room is barricaded with steel inches thick.'

'Where's K-9?'

'I thought he was following on.' Kimus looked shifty. 'His batteries are exhausted from trying to burn down the door.'

I'll bet they are, thought the Doctor grimly. He took one look at the group assembled around him. One Time Lady, a local who was proving quite a good shot, half a rebel, and a group of hobbled telepaths. Well, this would have to do.

'Kimus, you and Mula fall back to the Trophy Room. With a bit of luck, the Guards will be a bit careful about firing in there.' He pointed to the Mentiads. 'The rest of us, we're going to get to the engines.'

Behind them, Mula fired her weapon at the crumbling base of one of the huge statues. It toppled, the cruel face of Queen Xanxia shattering as it struck the ground, covering the escape route.

'Good work,' The Doctor gathered himself together and prepared to make a run for it.

Romana leaned over and whispered in his ear. 'What are we going to do, Doctor?'

'I don't know,' the Doctor whispered. Then he grinned, and darted off.

Chapter Eleven

Dinner with Newton

K-9 was stalled in front of the doors to the mighty Engine Room of Zanak. He tried raising his head at the approach of the Doctor's party down the corridor, but the most he could manage was a feeble twitch of his tail.

'Master …' the dog whispered.

The Doctor sprang at the floor, patting the dog with genuine concern. 'K-9!'

Again, the tail twitched. 'Batteries … My … Exhausted … Nearly … Are …'

'That's all right.' The Doctor used his most coaxing tones. He gestured to the Mentiads. 'The Mentiads can open the door if you can set up counter-interference on the psychic plane. Wavelength 338.79 microbars. Can you do that?' The Doctor peered at his dog encouragingly. 'Go on.'

'Negative … Master,' the dog croaked. 'Recharge I … imperative it is.'

'That's all right, K9.' The Doctor patted his dying dog on the head. 'You're still my best friend.' He looked over at Romana and shrugged sadly.

'Mas … Ter …' The dog's head slumped forward and he whispered something in a pathetic electronic gurgle.

The Doctor bent forward to listen and then slumped back on his heels. The dog's lights went out and his tail fell.

'Oh, K-9,' the Doctor sighed.

'What did he say?' asked Romana.

'He said …' The Doctor looked miserable. 'He said there's a power cable right behind me.' He leaped to his feet and yanked the cable from a power point. 'Quick! Open his inspection hatch,' he commanded.

Romana took the cable from the Doctor and plugged it into the robot. The air filled with sparks. The dog jolted and his head shot up, his eyes glowing a little too brightly. He made a low growling noise and lurched forward.

'Master?' snapped K-9, perhaps rather rapidly.

'Splendid!' The Doctor ignored the smell of burning wire. 'Now, K-9, can you divert any of this power into your frequency projectors?'

'Affirmative, Master,' the dog announced proudly. The air filled with a gentle buzzing which made the Doctor's teeth itch.

Pralix and the Mentiads shared a nervous smile. 'It's clearing, Doctor, it's clearing!'

'Good boy, K-9,' the Doctor stroked the dog affectionately. 'Has it cleared enough to open a door?'

The Mentiads frowned and stared at the engine room door. Nothing happened.

'More power, K-9!'

The buzzing grew and Romana saw dots behind her eyes.

The Mentiads looked at the door harder. Pralix emitted a single groan. 'We're not strong enough.'

Romana had a thought. 'Remember when we first tried to materialise on Calufrax?'

'Yes?' The Doctor didn't have time for distractions.

'We couldn't because Zanak was trying to materialise in the same place,' Romana coaxed patiently.

'And?' the Doctor snapped, and then his face lit up. 'And! If we couldn't materialise then neither can Zanak. We can pull the same trick! Back to the TARDIS!' He raced away, then stopped and doubled back, handing out jobs like he was running a village fête. Obviously, the Doctor had never tried running a village fête. The results would have been disastrous. 'K-9, keep generating power. Pralix, read my mind.'

The Mentiad frowned. 'Yes.'

'What can you see?'

Pralix frowned harder. Was this somehow the key to saving his people? 'A strip of metal.'

'Go on.'

'Subdivided at one end with an acute angle halfway along.'

'Perfect!' The Doctor patted him on the shoulder. 'Now, whatever happens, you keep concentrating on my mind. Come on, Romana. We've got a planet to save.'

The Time Lords picked a path through the ruined hall and stood waiting for the lift.

'What were you thinking of, Doctor?' asked Romana.

'A bent fork.'

'And why should anyone want to bend a fork?'

The Doctor fished around for an answer. 'I haven't the vaguest idea.'

People were handing Mr Fibuli reports like birthday cards. The Bridge was a hive of activity. None of the crew knew what was going on, who was in charge, why they were under attack, but they did know one thing. They knew how to start up the planet's engines, and they were throwing themselves into it.

'Captain, sir!' Mr Fibuli called.

For a moment, no one answered. The Nurse sat on her throne; the Captain stood rigidly by her side. Mr Fibuli was unsure about royalty – did one address them directly? He went to the Captain's side and whispered. 'Captain, sir—'

The Nurse glanced at him. 'Mr Fibuli?'

'Er …' Mr Fibuli looked between the two of them miserably. 'Dematerialisation in four minutes.'

'And what of the Doctor?' the Nurse asked rather too casually.

Mr Fibuli tried not to worry about his part in the Time Lord's escape. 'He's been sighted heading down the mountain.'

'Ah.' The Nurse smiled. 'He's running away.'

The Doctor and Romana were zipping along the inertia-less corridor. Romana had grown used to it as a way of travel, and looked forward to writing a little paper on its merits some day. She looked over her shoulder to check a pet theory about the effect of inertia on perspective. What she saw alarmed her.

'Doctor,' she cried. 'Look out!'

'I always hate it when people say that,' murmured the Doctor.

'Guards!' she shouted.

'I hate it when people say that too.'

The Guards started firing on them. Romana considered this ill-advised in an inertia-less environment as the energy bolts emerged sluggishly from the Guards' barrels and weaved their way erratically towards them. How curious. If she wasn't killed by them, there might be a short paper on the subject.

'Cover your head!' the Doctor ordered, throwing himself into a gliding crouch. 'We're almost there.'

The energy bolts passed drunkenly over their heads, reached the end of the corridor, and smashed the doorway apart. The Doctor tumbled off the corridor in what began as a forward roll and ended as more of a Swiss roll. Romana grabbed him, desperate to make for the door, but the Doctor's attention was caught by the control panel.

'Come on, Doctor!'

'Now, wait a minute.' The Doctor held up a hand, like a wise traffic warden. 'The Inertia Neutraliser. I think the conservation of momentum is a very important law in physics, don't you?'

'Yes.'

'And I don't think anyone should tamper with it, do you?'

'Why no.' Romana agreed solemnly.

The Doctor yanked a wire from the Inertia Neutraliser.

The two Guards reached the end of the corridor, and carried on, sailing through the air and thudding impressively into the door beyond, which creaked slowly open.

'Newton's revenge,' the Doctor announced.

As always, Mr Fibuli had a new problem. 'Captain, sir …'

'Yes?' cooed the Nurse.

The Captain winced. 'Speak, Mr Fibuli!'

Wringing his hands with embarrassment, Mr Fibuli gestured over to the Psychic Interferometer. 'Your device. There seems to be something counter-jamming it. It could affect the engines.'

'What?' The Captain staggered over, plugging himself into the device to check the horror for himself. 'We dematerialise in three minutes!' He grabbed a microphone. 'All Guards on alert! Someone is using a Psychic Interferometer counter-jamming frequency projector! Find it and destroy it!'

'Captain, sir,' Mr Fibuli purred with silken worry. 'Do you suppose any of the Guards know what a Psychic Interferometer counter-jamming frequency projector looks like?'

The Captain shrugged. It had been a long day. 'Guards!' he bellowed into the microphone. 'Destroy everything!' He turned back to Mr Fibuli with a gleam of devilment in his eyes.

The Mentiads stood in front of the Engine Room door, pouring all their power into it. It stayed exactly where it was. From behind it came the terrible roar as the Captain's machinery bellowed into a life even louder than its creator's.

The Doctor and Romana were in an air-car. The sky around them was crackling and fizzing with ozone as the engines of Zanak powered up.

'Who's Newton?' asked Romana, as she definitely wasn't going to talk about the sky.

'Old Isaac? Friend of mine on Earth.' The Doctor winced. He wondered what Isaac Newton would make of finding himself devoured by Zanak. He would probably send the Captain a pithy letter. 'Newton discovered gravity. Well, I say *discovered*. I had to give him a bit of a prod.'

'What did you do?' Romana narrowed her eyes.

'Climbed up a tree.'

'And?'

'Dropped an apple on his head.'

'Ah!' Romana nodded. 'And so that's how he discovered gravity.'

'Well no,' the Doctor admitted. 'He told me to clear off out of his tree. I had to explain gravity to him afterwards over dinner.'

Seeing as the Doctor had just admitted to breaking at least two laws of time, Romana changed the subject. 'Is that the TARDIS down there?'

'Yes!' The Doctor altered course for it.

'We'll never make it in time!' yelled Romana.

So the Doctor threw them into a dive.

With the last of the Guards ranged against them picked off, Kimus and Mula proudly joined the Mentiads at the engine room door. They were worried to find it was still closed and even more worried to find no Doctor in sight.

'Where is the Doctor?' asked Kimus.

Pralix gave him a tired smile. 'I'm concentrating on the Doctor's mind. Do not disturb me.'

'Oh,' Kimus muttered. 'Why?'

'We're still too weak to move the door.' Pralix's smile vanished as though it was too much effort.

K-9 rolled forward, wisps of smoke leaking from his mouth, giving him an endearingly rakish air. 'My counter-jamming field is increasing … slowly.'

'So the door will soon be open?' Mula asked, trying to sound hopeful.

From behind the doors came a metallic bellow from the great engines.

Kimus realised they weren't going to be in time.

The Doctor threw himself at the TARDIS console so enthusiastically Romana was amazed it didn't squeak in alarm. Tugging at levers and twisting switches, his tone was that of a man soaring over Niagara Falls in a bathtub. 'Don't take it personally, old girl, just try and survive.'

Romana went to pick up the TARDIS manual, thought better of it, and kicked it firmly out of the way. This was a time when the Doctor needed practical help.

'Earth coordinates?' he asked.

'5804-4684-884.' As she called them out, he punched them in. The Doctor's method of flying his ship might not be orthodox but it was certainly brisk.

'Multiloop Stabiliser set, Synchronic Feedback ... on ...'

'If we're going to try and materialise at exactly the same point in time and space, how do we know when to do it?' Romana asked. 'It only happened as a fluke the first time.'

The Doctor stopped muttering, and looked up at her. 'Very good point. Zanak could start dematerialising any second now ... We've got to be spot on.' He shrugged sheepishly. 'You'll have to monitor the Warp Oscilloscope and Gravity Dilation Meters ... They'll both peak when Zanak switches from dematerialisation mode to rematerialisation mode. And then ...'

'Yes?'

'Brace yourself.'

The Nurse was impatiently gripping the arms of the Captain's chair. 'How soon, Captain, how soon?' she cried without looking away from the skies beyond the dome. 'This waiting is intolerable! We must jump, we simply must jump!'

The Captain spoke with the wounded dignity of an abused butler. 'We are now ready.'

'Then jump! Jump instantly!'

The Captain heaved himself towards the controls, and tugged them into some kind of order. 'Planet Terra, star system Sol, galactic coordinates 5804-4684-884, surround jump commences in five seconds. Four ... Three ...'

As he counted down, the Nurse watched fire spread across the mountain, pouring into the air around them and then boiling up into the clouds. The funnel of light spread across the sky, wrapping itself around the entire planet, making ready to lob it into time-space.

'Now, Doctor, dematerialise now!' Romana called as the planet Zanak vanished.

For a moment, a strange blue box hung on its own in space, just where the planet Calufrax had once been. Then it also vanished.

There was a small fire on the console. The Doctor patted at it casually with the end of his scarf. 'Going well so far,' he said.

The entire ship was shuddering, and thick black smoke began to pour from the roundels in the walls as the TARDIS lurched like a pedalo heading into a hurricane.

Mr Fibuli looked up from a screen, sucking at the end of a pen. 'Captain – there was a slight disturbance on the Warp Oscilloscope during dematerialisation.'

'Monitor it,' the Captain cautioned.

The Nurse stared raptly through the dome at the dizzying whirl of stars above the planet's surface.

The Captain reached over to a control and, with an expert's touch, tweaked it just a little. 'Monitor it, and prepare for rematerialisation. Surrounding Planet Terra in five seconds ...'

Over at galactic coordinates 5804-4684-884, the planet Earth was enjoying a splendid day being the third planet out from the sun. It hadn't been invaded for a few days now.

All that was about to change.

'Rematerialisation commence!' called Romana.

The Doctor did nothing.

'Now, Doctor!'

The Doctor looked up. 'Oh, right,' he said, and pulled the materialisation lever.

The TARDIS hurled itself out of the Space-Time Vortex.

TARDISes do not speak. Or, if they do, we live too quickly to listen.

But, as the TARDIS hurtled out of the Space-Time Vortex to save the planet Earth, it allowed itself to say one thing.

'Wheeeeeeeeeee!'

*

156

A shadow wrapped itself around the planet Earth. The shadow began to squeeze.

And then, somewhere inside the darkness, a small blue box popped up. It was such a little thing, really. Especially if you were a shadow wrapping yourself around a planet. Barely even a dot.

But as soon as the dot arrived, really very bad things started to happen.

Mr Fibuli's world was shaking itself apart. He could hear the screaming across the Bridge and knew things were not going well.

The Captain strode across his Bridge, sweeping people aside as he took over their controls. He was flying the entire planet single-handed. 'Mr Fibuli. It is happening again!'

The Nurse turned from the view. Below her was the planet Earth, a blue-green globe wearing a veil of cloud. The planet was ringed with a fierce red glow as Zanak tried to get a grip on it.

'What's happening, Captain?'

The Captain did not even look up from the controls. 'It's the Doctor's vessel. He's trying to materialise in the same space as us.'

Mr Fibuli managed to make sense of a readout and wished he hadn't. 'Every circuit's jamming.'

The Captain roared with frustration.

*

Romana tried to read a dial, but the glass cracked and smoke puffed from it. The whole TARDIS was shaking and the air seemed to be on fire.

'Doctor! There's no way we can survive this!'

She suddenly realised why the Doctor had a scarf. He'd looped it around the central column and was using it as a seatbelt. She'd never have told him this, but right now, he looked just a little magnificent.

'It's getting worse!' She felt the lever she was clinging to bend a little and she really hoped it didn't do anything important.

The Doctor, of all things, smiled at her. 'And it'll carry on getting worse until one of us explodes ... unless the Mentiads get that door open!'

He threw back his head and shrieked a single word: 'Pralix!'

'What are you doing?' cried Romana.

'Shhh!' the Doctor counselled. 'I'm opening a communications channel.'

Things were not calm outside the Engine Room. The Mentiads poured their souls into the Engine Room door, willing it to give way while trying to ignore the multidimensional scream swamping their minds.

Pralix looked up, and he almost – almost – grinned.

'Pralix! Can you hear me?' The Doctor's voice sang into his head from a long way away.

Pralix nodded. 'Brothers. The Doctor is trying to reach me. We must concentrate together. The voice is too faint for me to hear.'

Aboard the TARDIS the Doctor slapped the side of his head several times. 'There's just so much background noise,' he sighed.

Romana tightened her grip on an unhappy-looking dial and wondered when they were going to die.

'Romana!' the Doctor cried with delight.

'Yes?' she said weakly.

'Switch off the TARDIS force fields.'

Oh, now he'd gone too far.

'What? But, that's madness. The shields are the only protection we've got.'

'All the same,' the Doctor agreed. 'Turn them off.'

Romana hesitated. Two days ago she'd had a bright future in temporal academia. Was she really going to throw it away for a planet she'd never heard of? Her eyes wandered to the TARDIS manual and then snapped back to the Doctor's face. Never mind all she'd learned.

Of course she was throwing her lot in with the Doctor.

She reached over to the controls. 'It's been nice knowing you, Doctor.'

'And you,' he replied.

*

Romana turned off the TARDIS shields. The noise and shaking instantly got worse. The ship dropped like a broken lift. Circuits blew across the entire console. Smoke poured from the ceiling.

But, in good news, Pralix's voice echoed much more clearly in their heads. So loud, you could barely hear the TARDIS's shrieks of excited alarm.

'Doctor,' said Pralix. 'Are you there? What's happening?'

With the TARDIS shields down, there was nothing to stop the arrival of Zanak. The pirate planet squeezed itself a little more into corporeality, a shadow solidifying around the Earth and pushing the Moon out of the way. The problem was that there were now two quasi-solid objects trying to materialise around the planet Earth simultaneously, and with the shields off there was little to divide the TARDIS's extremely finite exterior from its theoretically infinite interior. Freed from its confines, the inside of the TARDIS rushed against the planet Zanak like a tidal wave surging from a matchbox.

The vast engines of Zanak cried out.

'Oh Captain!' wailed Mr Fibuli. 'It's getting worse! We must abandon the jump!' he begged.

The crew had all been thrown to the floor. The Nurse stood at the dome, staring into the melting sky beyond.

Her hands were grasping the rail and the knuckles were white.

'More power, Captain!' she screamed. 'More power!'

As impossible shapes filled the atmosphere above the Earth, the air of the planet below filled with a noise that no one would forget.

A terrible wheezing, groaning sound …

The Doctor was trying to keep his voice calm. Realising he was clenching one of his hands, he jammed it casually in his coat pocket.

All around him, the TARDIS walls buckled and warped. Hovering in the thick air in front of them, was the image of Pralix's head, frowning.

'Doctor,' it said. 'Are you all right?'

'Oh, perfectly,' the Doctor lied in a tone that said cucumber sandwiches were even now being served. Out of the corner of his eye he saw Romana was using a fire extinguisher on the Gravitic Anomaliser. 'Now, Pralix, please tell me you have enough power to lift that door?'

Pralix shook his holographic head. 'No, Doctor. Our minds are so weak we couldn't lift anything bigger than a spanner!'

'A spanner?' The Doctor boggled at the hologram. 'A spanner! That's it! Bung a spanner in the works.'

'What?'

'Pralix! Forget the door, can you project your minds beyond it?'

The shimmering image of Pralix frowned at this notion.

This was all very well thought Romana, but the fire extinguisher was now empty and there was an awful lot more fire to go. 'Doctor, the TARDIS is about to explode!'

Pralix frowned. The Mentiads frowned. They took their energy, the life force of dead worlds, and pushed their way past the great bulkhead, their minds' eyes floating beyond into the mighty Engine Room.

The crew may have deserted the vast engines of Zanak, but the caverns were filled with the pounding energy, the screaming of metal, and the howling of alarms. A palpable force, somewhere between psychic, telepathic and terribly sad, prowled around these vast engines

The Mentiads' life force weaved between the fearsome pistons that pounded creation and quantum physics into submission.

'Doctor! Our minds are now in the Engine Room. Can you see?'

The Doctor mentally re-walked his earlier tour of the room.

'I think,' he announced casually, 'that if you look over there on the right, you'll find a lovely spanner lying on the floor.'

The Mentiads focused on a small spanner – the one the Doctor had left behind earlier. It twitched, and then lifted up into the air.

'Wonderful!' the Doctor said. The TARDIS controls he was gripping were now uncomfortably hot. But, from the genteel tone of his voice, he could have been sipping lemonade by a stream. 'On your left, you'll see a Macrovectoid Particle Analyser, go straight on past the Omnimodular Thermocron over there! And what do we have here? Why, it's the Megaphoton Discharge Link!'

'But what do we do?' asked Pralix as the spanner paused in mid air.

'Hit it, of course.'

The spanner hovered in mid-air, hesitant, curiously polite.

'Hit it!' the Doctor shouted.

The spanner fell, smashing down on the Megaphoton Discharge Link.

There was a small blast of fire. Little more than a pop. Then another one. A little bigger. Then another, bigger still.

And then the mighty engines of Zanak, the biggest warp engines the universe had ever known, exploded.

Chapter Twelve

The Captain's Plan

The spectacular explosion blew the top off the great mountain. Fire shot up into the air, and rubble began to fall from the sky. Not precious stones, metals or gems, but rocks and lava, falling in a burning, choking hail on the terrified people of Zanak.

The Doctor laughed like a madman on a burning rollercoaster as his time machine melted faster than a watch on Salvador Dali's barbeque.

Mr Fibuli screamed as the blast hit the Bridge. The noise was terrifying. The shaft to the planet's empty heart blew open, a pillar of flame leaping from it. Every single alarm shrieked as the view through the dome went from a whirling blue void to a strange, empty whiteness.

The Captain cried out – whether in fear or in rage at the death of his engines, Mr Fibuli never knew.

The Nurse howled in fury, gripping the prow as the vast, glass window exploded around her. She held her ground, even as the entire planet plunged into a nosedive. Mr Fibuli, dangling over a terrible drop, screamed and grabbed desperately at a desk.

All of a sudden, the world went quiet.

The alarms stopped.

The vast engines of Zanak had fallen forever silent.

'Actually,' said Mr Fibuli, 'we're going to be all right.'

They were to be his last words.

Zanak was, for a quantum moment, nowhere. The noble, howling blue box gave one last roar, glowed bright, then let go. Zanak, stretched through time and space like an elastic band, was released. Unable to stabilise itself around the Earth, it shot back into the Vortex.

The TARDIS was dark and still. Distant creaks echoed through the halls like the complaints of decrepit relatives.

Pleased and surprised to find himself alive, the Doctor opened an eye.

'You can never relax for a moment in this job,' he announced to the smoking ruins of his time machine.

Romana pulled herself up from the floor. 'We've done it.'

'The question is, will we ever be able to do anything else again?' The Doctor found his feet, and wobbled towards the control pillar. All the lights on it were out, apart from a single glow coming from somewhere deep inside it. He flicked a switch. Nothing happened. So he flicked another one. There were still plenty to go. One of them would do something. Surely.

'We should get back and see if someone's still alive on Zanak. Shall we try and materialise?'

Romana shrugged. She tried picking some of the soot from her hair and then gave up. 'I suppose it can't do any more harm.'

Zanak had arrived somewhere. The sky above it was unpromising, with just a single sun, but the planet was in one piece. For the moment. The stresses and strains of its recent contortion had pressed down on its thin crust. The great metal bulwarks underneath shivered and split. Cracks spread across the surface. Sand poured down through the gaps. The planet began to fall into itself.

The world was quiet. Even the ruins of the mountain were silent. Apart from in a single chamber, where a small blue box crawled painfully out of thin air.

'Good grief.' Romana wrinkled her nose in disgust.

Stepping out of the TARDIS, the Doctor made to pat the ship and clearly thought better of it. He took in their surroundings. Ooh. Not bad.

'The Throne Room of Queen Xanxia.'

'Is that her?' Romana stared at the repellently ancient figure shrivelled onto the chair.

'That's her, the old harpy.' The Doctor pulled a face at the ancient queen. The remains did not react.

Romana, feeling impetuous, stuck her tongue out. Then she prodded one of the pillars. 'It's a pity we can't just switch her off,' she announced before the Doctor did anything hasty.

'Wouldn't dream of it,' the Doctor promised. 'Any interference in the Time Dam Field would trigger an explosion that would blast us off what's left of this planet.'

Romana pursed her lips. 'And I'm guessing the same happens if the power supply fails.'

'Which, given that I've nobbled Zanak, is now an inevitability,' the Doctor confessed.

'Well, then, what do we do?'

The Doctor was always surprised when he considered his options, mostly to find that he had any.

'I think we adapt the Captain's plan.'

'The Captain's plan?'

'Oh yes.' The Doctor made a final face at Old Queen Xanxia and headed off. 'The Captain's always had a plan.'

The Nurse should have been dead: she had been impaled by a heavy girder when the ceiling had collapsed. No matter. She simply rearranged her molecules and stood up, checking her black box for damage.

Things were bad. But it was not the end. It would never be the end for Queen Xanxia.

The view from the shattered window showed only stars. A thin, cold wind swept in, sending shredded reports fluttering up into the air.

'Captain!' she called.

There was no reply.

'Captain?' She felt a moment's worry. Was everyone else dead?

Then she heard a strange noise. She edged her way past the shattered workings of the flight computer, and saw the Captain hunched on the floor dragging a tiny bundle from under a pile of rubble. The noise was coming from the Captain. He was crying.

'Mr Fibuli.' He pointed to the limp figure crushed under the ceiling. 'Dead. He was a good man.' With a sigh, he took Mr Fibuli's glasses off, and stood stiffly. His robotic arm flopped weakly to one side, fluid leaking from an elbow joint. His faceplate was dented, and his human eye was swollen almost shut. As he moved towards the Nurse, his left leg dragged and rattled.

With an effort, he focused his damaged eye on her. 'They're all dead,' he said, gesturing to the bodies scattered across the Bridge.

The Nurse snapped her fingers. 'Pull yourself together, Captain. We can still triumph. Make some repairs.'

The Captain lurched over to a control panel, placed Mr Fibuli's glasses on it, and got back to work. When he spoke, his voice was so low it could just have been the hissing of his ruptured hydraulics. 'Somehow, Mr Fibuli, you shall be avenged.'

The Doctor was showing Romana the Captain's Trophy Room. She took in the planets held in their casings and, to his surprise, whistled. 'It's a masterpiece of gravitic geometry.'

The Doctor nodded encouragingly. 'Isn't it?'

Romana peered at Calufrax now wobbling in its case and she frowned. Something was wrong here.

'All the forces cancel each other out perfectly,' the Doctor was continuing. 'Otherwise ...' He made a child's sound for a giant explosion. Pleased, he made the noise again.

'The Captain's plan!' Romana had already got the point. 'How clever of the Captain. He built this under her nose?'

'The bang will be so big, calling this a bomb doesn't even begin to do it justice,' the Doctor agreed.

'So all that shouting and blustering was just an act to lull Xanxia into a false sense of security while he built this?'

'Exactly!' the Doctor boomed. 'Let that be a lesson to you, my girl. Never take anyone at face value, no matter how foolish they seem.'

Was the Doctor trying to make a point about himself? Romana wondered. Well, she'd make up her own mind on that one.

*

The Nurse regarded the Captain. Her old pet clanked and hissed away. He assured her he could bring life back to the engines, summon up some power. Just enough. People kept telling her there was never enough. But there always was. Power to defeat the Mentiads, to devour more planets, to keep going.

The human side of the Captain's face was drooping. The poor old thing was falling apart. But then again, not everyone was like her. She was lucky. No one else got to be Queen Xanxia.

'Hurry, Captain! Hurry!' she called over to him.

He put a circuit board down with a slam and glared at her. His hand wandered jerkily against the Psychic Interferometer. Perhaps it was just an accident.

Mula and Kimus had made their way to the Bridge door, trying to open it. It appeared the Captain was sealed in. Even K-9's blaster couldn't dent it.

'It's no use,' Kimus sighed. They'd come so far, but there was no opening it.

There was a cough behind them. It was Pralix. Behind him stood the Mentiads.

'We Mentiads must try to open it,' he said, and he smiled.

The Mentiads nodded. 'Brothers, our strength is increasing. This time we shall succeed.'

*

The Doctor and Romana were discussing the Captain's plan. The Doctor was adamant. 'We must be able to adapt it somehow.'

'But the Captain will have the controls on the Bridge,' Romana said, not fancying the Doctor tampering with any of the trophy cabinets. It was one thing to blow up Queen Xanxia. It was another to blow themselves up too. 'Wait a minute,' she said. 'The only way the Captain could destroy Xanxia without blowing himself and this whole mountain to atoms would be to get inside the perimeter of the Time Dams without disturbing them. Which would require astronomic energy sources.'

The Doctor gestured around the Trophy Room. 'Here they are, all perfectly balanced out.'

'So this isn't just a weapon – he was collecting planets until he had enough of them. And all he has to do to get inside the Time Dams is to alter the balance slightly and create a standing vortex in the middle of the time field, so time starts up at the normal speed and the Queen dies?'

'Right!'

'It's brilliant!' Romana enthused in a way that made the Doctor feel mildly jealous. 'But I don't see how it helps us.'

'Well …' The Doctor played his trump card casually. 'It wouldn't have worked anyway.'

'Why not? The theory's sound enough.'

'Yes, but Calufrax isn't.' The Doctor marched over to the shrunken relic's display case and knocked on it politely. 'This is not a normal planet. It's an artificially metricised structure consisting of a substance with a variable atomic weight.'

The penny dropped very loudly in Romana's head. 'You mean that Calufrax, the entire planet … ?'

' … was the second segment of the Key to Time.' The Doctor waved at it. 'Hello!'

'Of course! No wonder the Tracer kept going mad.' Romana wrinkled her nose. She tried to ignore the sick feeling in her stomach.

'Try it now,' the Doctor suggested.

'The Locatormutor Core? On the remains?' Romana's worry shifted to panic as she felt around in her flowing dress.

'The Tracer,' the Doctor urged. 'You *have* still got it?'

'I thought *you* had it!' Romana went through her pockets again, but ball gowns did not have many pockets.

'Oh,' sighed the Doctor. He rummaged in his coat and pulled out the Tracer. 'There we are. You should be more careful with it, you know.'

Romana took it from him and waved it at Calufrax. There was a loud crackle. 'But we can't remove Calufrax,' she said. 'We can't move anything here. If we do, we'll just upset the whole system, create a gravity whirlpool, and destroy Zanak.'

'Not if I do something immensely clever,' grinned the Doctor. 'Let's go find the others.'

The Mentiads were staring at the door to the Bridge and it was starting to buckle.

'Hello everyone,' the Doctor said, reappearing with Romana. 'I like what we've done to the place.'

He went to shake Pralix by the hand, then noticed the quivering door.

'It all comes down to this in the end, once all the shouting and cruelty are over. Doesn't matter if it's a castle, a bunker, or the cockpit of a broken pirate ship: this is where it always ends. Sealed up like a tin of pilchards. A tin of panicking pilchards. Planning one final desperate move.' He turned back to the Mentiads, to Mula, Kimus, Romana and the robot dog. 'Let's put a stop to it.'

The Captain wired up one last circuit board and slotted it into place. The deck started to hum with power. The Captain smiled, his human hand stroking the remains of the Polyphase Avatron. He'd found the golden scrap among the wreckage and placed it on the desk so that it could watch. Pretty Polly, he thought. She'd have liked this.

The Nurse rushed over to him. 'Have you done it? Is it ready?'

'Yes, Xanxia. At last I am ready.' The Captain turned around to face her. He leaned back in his chair, and concentrated on cleaning Mr Fibuli's spectacles.

The Nurse paused. She never liked anyone's tone, but she suddenly and particularly disliked the Captain's. A nagging question formed in her mind. And then she noticed the door to the Bridge opening. She howled in alarm as the rebel army surged in. Rebels, on her Bridge! 'Do something!'

'I already have.' The Captain stood and faced her. They were all here. Here at the end. Even the Doctor and the girl and the robot dog. Well then, they could watch, and they could marvel. And then they could die with him.

The Captain held up the trigger he'd been building. It was ready.

'I shall be free from you, you hag.'

The Doctor was yelling that it would not work. But then, what did the Doctor know? What had any of them ever known? The Captain made to stab down on the trigger. But his damaged arm would not work. Hydraulic fluid sputtered from the elbow.

The Captain summoned the last of his strength, but the Nurse got there first, and gave the dial on her black box a vicious twist. The Captain froze, mid lunge, a horrid croak coming from his throat.

The Captain's agonised eye rolled helplessly in his paralysed body, twisting as first smoke and then fire guttered from the joints of his mighty frame. His remaining hand twitched helplessly, desperate to reach the console. Then his body vanished in flames.

For a moment, the figure of the Captain stood there, and then the burning figure toppled forward across the desk, coming to rest by the broken Polyphase Avatron.

The Nurse turned to face the rebels, the Mentiads and the Doctor. There wasn't a trace of fear in her eyes.

'And now it's your turn,' she sneered, holding up her black box. Energy was spitting from it.

'No please, I can explain,' the Doctor begged.

'No Doctor, never again,' the Nurse twisted the black box.

Which was when Kimus shot her.

You can't shoot holograms, of course. But the energy beam disrupted the projection of the Nurse, and also took out the black box. Her body flickered, wobbled, and then solidified. She threw back her head and was about to laugh when one of the badly dressed, shabby Mentiads blocked her path. Tiresome.

'Never again,' said Pralix to his queen.

As one, the Mentiads stepped forward and stared at the Nurse, and the combined life force of so many worlds drained out of them and into her.

The horror, the misery, the torment – everything she had brought about – the billions of lives she had swept away, the eternity of stolen sunsets and uprooted trees, the raging souls of a dozen dozen planets fell on the Nurse and she faded away, screaming.

The Mentiads listened to the scream lingering on for a long time. And then they all broke into radiant grins.

Mula regarded the Captain's body. 'Are they dead?'

'Well, the Captain certainly is, but Xanxia's another matter.' The Doctor looked around the creaking remains of the Captain's ship. 'You'd all better get out of here. This place is pretty unstable. Get down to the foot of the mountain.'

'What about you?' asked Kimus.

'It's all right, We'll follow on later. Off you go.' The Doctor shooed them away.

Soon the Doctor and Romana were alone. The Doctor was idly stroking the bent tin wings of the Captain's pet. Through the shattered glass of the prow, the long night was coming to a close, and the first shades of dawn were breaking through the sky.

The Doctor was thinking things carefully through.

'So,' he said after a very long pause. 'This might be a bit tricky. Romana, take K-9 back to the TARDIS and wait for me there.'

'What about you?' Romana was worried he was going to blow something up.

'I've got a couple of things to tidy up here,' he said evasively.

Romana frowned. He was definitely going to blow something up.

Once she was back in the TARDIS, Romana was philosophical. Leaving the Doctor alone with the largest bomb in creation was like leaving a child alone with a toy and expecting them not to play with it.

The only good thing was that, with the doors shut, maybe the TARDIS would stand a chance of surviving the blast.

K-9 had offered to calculate the odds of that happenstance, but Romana had swiftly declined. Instead they'd got to work on patching up the damage to the controls. After all, they might need to leave in a hurry.

The TARDIS doors opened, and Romana flinched.

The Doctor strode in, hands in pockets, whistling.

'What have you done, Doctor?'

'You'd never believe it.'

'Try me.'

The Doctor went over to the controls and started coaxing some remaining life from them.

'Doctor!' called Romana again.

'All right!' The Doctor held up a hand in friendly surrender. He summoned up, from who knew where, a remote image of Zanak on the screen, hanging in space. 'The Captain's engines are destroyed. Zanak's not going anywhere. It's also unstable.' He pointed to cracks appearing in the planet's crust. 'The Captain's Trophy Room is also on the point of collapse. The resulting explosion could wipe out this system, and wake up the neighbours.'

This did not sound good.

'However!' The Doctor brightened. 'I've switched the Captain's circuits around to create a hyperspatial force shield around the shrunken planets, and put his dematerialisation controls into remote mode.'

'So we can operate them from here?' Romana was baffled.

'Exactly.'

'Clever,' she admitted. 'But I don't see how that helps.'

'You don't?' The Doctor looked for reassurance from K-9, but the dog was recharging tactfully. 'Well, first I dematerialise the TARDIS, then I make Zanak dematerialise for a millisecond or two, then I invert the gravity field of the hyperspatial force shield and drop the shrunken planets into the hollow centre of Zanak.'

Romana was stunned. 'What then?'

'Well, I would have thought that was perfectly obvious. With the compression field removed, the remains of the planets will expand in an instant to fill the hollow space. Zanak will be saved.'

'And Calufrax?'

The Doctor was as casual as a fish and chip supper. 'Well, naturally, I'll fling Calufrax off into the Space-Time Vortex and we pick it up later in the TARDIS.'

'I do think that's cheating,' said Romana, but she couldn't resist grinning.

'Showmanship,' shrugged the Doctor.

'It's quite ingenious,' she conceded.

'*Quite ingenious?* It's brilliant. It's fantastic!' The Doctor was already dancing around the controls of his ship, getting it ready to do something impossible.

'Fine, it's fantastic.'

'You're terribly kind.' The Doctor bowed graciously, then engaged the dematerialisation circuits. 'Here we go then …'

In the ruins of the Captain's ship, the trophy cabinets containing his most prized possessions glowed.

A moment later, they were empty.

In the empty heart of the planet Zanak, things were quiet. The vast engines, the awesome mining galleries were stilled. The only sound was a tectonic creaking as the planet's surface shifted uneasily.

And then came a rushing sound as a dozen planets appeared from nowhere and suddenly had everywhere to be.

*

Sat inside her Time Dams, Queen Xanxia waited out eternity. She was dimly aware that things had not been going well, but there would be plenty of time to start again. There always would be. Nothing could ever stop Queen Xanxia.

'Congratulations,' said Romana, just about managing to keep the surprise out of her voice. The hyperspace force field had contained the expansion and Zanak hadn't split open like an egg. Some people really did have all the luck. But, wait –

'Haven't you forgotten something?'

'Me?' The Doctor was shocked at the very idea.

'What about the Bridge, and the Time Dams?'

The Doctor deflected this. 'Let's ask K-9.'

The robot dog wagged his tail happily. He knew his Master.

'Piece of cake, Master. Blow them up.'

'Isn't that rather crude?' Romana felt she was fighting the inevitable.

'True, it's a bit crude,' the Doctor conceded. 'But it's immensely satisfying.'

Getting the TARDIS to make the short hop had been, the Doctor claimed, like taking a milk float grand prix racing, but the little blue box eventually chugged into being in the city's market square. Gathered there was quite a crowd. The young, the old, the Mentiads, and Mula and Kimus.

The Doctor brought out a remote control detonator. It was an old-fashioned plunger attached to a box labelled 'ACME'. He placed it ceremoniously in front of the people of Zanak.

Kimus stared at the plunger dubiously. 'When all this is over, will we really be free?'

'I don't see why not.' The Doctor glanced up at the smoking ruins of the Captain's mountain. 'It's entirely up to you. You've got to make this world a better place to live in. You've got plenty of material wealth …'

'But there are other things.' Mula smiled at him. She was going to make a better leader than Kimus. The Doctor wondered if Kimus had realised that yet.

'I think this is a good place in the universe to settle down, you know.' The Doctor had got Romana to do the research, of course. 'You've got a reasonable sun, good neighbours and some quite convenient stars for when you get round to ordinary space travel. I think you're going to be all right here.'

Mula nodded, which was a good thing, as the Doctor hadn't a clue what to do if they wanted to settle elsewhere.

He turned to the Mentiads. 'What I want to know is, am I going to blow up that mountain, or are you?'

Pralix stepped forward, speaking for the Mentiads now. The old leader nodded at him, his smile a fraction less sad. It was time for the Mentiads to make new beginnings too.

'We will destroy it, Doctor,' Pralix said. 'There is just enough life force left, I think, to depress that plunger. It seems a fitting way to expend it.'

The crowd nodded encouragement.

The Mentiads stood around the detonator. They seemed less pale, less gaunt, their faces almost unlined. They frowned, but it was a gentle, determined frown.

The plunger sank down.

A few seconds later the remains of the mountain, the mighty engines, Queen Xanxia, and the *Vantarialis*, the most feared pirate ship in the spaceways, all vanished in dust and flame.

The Mentiads stood back and laughed.

The crowd applauded.

And, if no diamonds rained from the sky that day, no one minded.

The Doctor turned to Romana. 'That was very satisfying, wasn't it?'

'Immensely,' Romana agreed.

'Come on.' The Doctor was already heading back to the TARDIS. 'Still four more pieces of the Key to Time out there. We've got a job to do.'

'Affirmative, Master,' K-9 said.

And the TARDIS fell away from Zanak and on to further adventures.

BBC

—ĐOCTOR WHO—

The Pirate Planet

If you have enjoyed this novelisation of the broadcast version of *The Pirate Planet*, you might enjoy *Doctor Who: The Pirate Planet* (ISBN 1849906785).

Based on Douglas Adams's much longer first draft scripts, it contains many more dead planets, the much fiddlier original ending to Part Three, startling information about the writer of the TARDIS manual, unexpected chickens, and Douglas Adams's original notes, along with various other plot strands and jokes that were lost for forty years.

Three times longer than this book, it can be used to stun an unloved relative.